WHEN BOBBY KENNEDY WAS A MOVING MAN

a novel by

Robert Ellis Gordon

Black Heron Press
Post Office Box 95676
Seattle, Washington 98145

When Bobby Kennedy Was a Moving Man is the winner of the 1993 King County Arts Commission Publication Award for Fiction.

This is a work of fiction. Except for some historical characters, any resemblance to persons living or dead is purely coincidental. The author has mythologized several historical characters; the reader should not expect their portrayal to conform to the behaviors depicted in some of their biographies.

ISBN 0-930773-27-6 (cloth)
ISBN 0-930773-28-4 (paper)

Published by:
    Black Heron Press
    Post Office Box 95676
    Seattle, Washington 98145

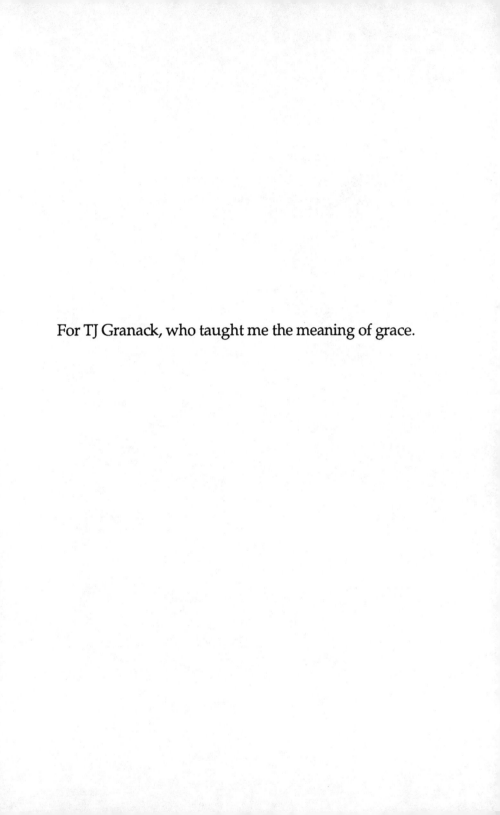

For TJ Granack, who taught me the meaning of grace.

ACKNOWLEDGMENTS

I wish to thank my literary agents, Neil Olson and Eric Ashworth, for their uncommon decency and patience.

In addition, I wish to thank good friend and colleague Thomas Lee Wright for his faith, generosity and penchant for keeping me reasonably honest.

For financial support and other gifts, I am deeply grateful to the King County Arts Commission; to my grandparents, William and Edith Gordon; to my parents, Mark and Joan Gordon and, especially, to Anita O. Kyte.

Finally, for everything in the world, thanks to friends and colleagues DJ Hamilton, Paul Potocki and Judith Roche.

A Note From the Author

From January through June of 1990, I, Stanley V. Higgins, a thirty-eight-year-old itinerant banjo player, bartender, roustabout, voracious reader (particularly of American labor history and any and all kinds of animal fables), one-time circus juggler, former merchant seaman, card sharp, counterfeiter, pickpocket, ranch hand, hedonist, penitent, recidivist, farm-implement salesman, and progressive Democrat in the tradition of Robert Marion LaFollette, Franklin Delano Roosevelt, Adlai Ewing Stevenson, and Robert Francis Kennedy, worked as a moving man for the Jake Fuller Moving Company in Seattle, Washington.

The company was of medium size, running an average of five trucks per day, and employing six full-timers and anywhere from zero to fifteen part-timers, depending on dispatching needs. While performing a mix of local office and household moves, I would estimate the percentage of the former to the latter to be as high as four or five to one. This emphasis on commercial clients, particularly banks, insurance companies, and the city's largest, most reputable law firms, reflected both Seattle's status as a burgeoning commercial center fortuitously located along the vital Pacific Rim trade route, and Jake Fuller's fine nose for profit. Or, to put it another way, the Jake Fuller Moving Company represented the gourmet end of the regional short-haul trade.

All of which would be of little consequence to the history of our times were it not for the fact that during my first three days on the job, Jake paired me with a fellow who was not only named Bobby Kennedy; and who not only bore an uncanny resemblance to the wiry and passionate, if somewhat tinny-voiced, blue-eyed hero of my youth, and who not only spoke in hauntingly familiar staccato rhythms that were punctuated by frequent chops of the hand, but who actually claimed to *be* the late senator himself. Moreover, as we traversed the city and its environs, picking up and dropping off loads of furniture, my sandy-haired partner told me an outrageous story regarding the one segment of Robert Kennedy's otherwise overly scrutinized past that had *not* been addressed by any of his numerous biographers. I refer, of course, to the indignities and tribulations he allegedly endured in the years following his premature death.

I will leave it to you to decide if the man's audacious chronicle seems plausible. Before I recede into the role of mere recorder, however—and before, it is hoped, my own credibility has been irreparably damaged in the minds of any readers who yet remain—let me state, emphatically, that my apparent erudition notwithstanding, I am no stranger to charlatans, poker cheats, desperadoes, flim-flam men, dashing bank robbers, homicidal maniacs, and almost every other type of rogue extant on the planet. In addition and regrettably, I myself am no stranger to the inside of penitentiaries. It therefore follows that, based upon my vast experience in a multitude of unsavory endeavors and situations, *I had more reason than most to spot this fellow for the fraud he assuredly was.*

Which is precisely what I did. During that first morning on the truck, I paid Bobby's outlandish claims no more heed than I would the irritating drone of a radio preacher soliciting funds to pay for his extramarital carnal pleasures. I looked out the window; I pretended to doze; I whistled old radio tunes from my hobo days; I straddled the line of vulgar impudence, in other words, in my attempts to discourage this bore from continuing with his inane prattle. And I was preparing myself to stray over that line—perhaps even to resort to the use of force—when Bobby brought about a sudden change in my attitude through the levitation of a solid oak dresser. Yes, you heard me correctly: a dresser. And yes it *was* (I double checked) solid oak.

This miracle occurred at approximately twelve forty-five p.m. as we were about to make our first post-lunch delivery. I remember standing on the sidewalk outside the customer's residence, a lavish, three-story rococo affair with several acres of beach front on the exlusive east shore of Lake Washington; I remember toying with the notion of burglarizing the place on some bleak moonless night in the not-too-distant future; I remember Bobby remarking, apropos of absolutely nothing I'd said, that a spread like this was undoubtedly choked with floodlights, alarms, and hidden cameras; I admit to feeling a rare twinge of shame when I realized he might be clairvoyant; I remember the sweet, salty after-taste of a recently ingested meal consisting of a Big Mac, medium fries, and a chocolate shake (a combination, incidentally, that Bobby Kennedy—lanky though he was—could never seem to get enough of, scarfing down three portions to my one every day that we worked together); I remember thinking, when I stared at the oak dresser—now shorn of its protective bubblewrap as it sat on the back of the truck—that once it had been an acorn; I remember the sound of a lone gardener's rake; I remember the odd way Bobby gazed at the dresser, affixing it with an affectionate and mildly secretive smile, the type of smile I later imagined he might've affixed to Marilyn Monroe after she'd made one of her kinkier suggestions; and I remember how, in defiance of the laws of Newton and God, the dresser seemed to follow Bobby's gaze as it rose several feet, hovered briefly above the truck bed, slid horizontally through the air, and floated down ever so gently until it came to rest atop a furniture pad we'd draped over a patch of sidewalk several minutes before. Whereupon my partner flashed a Kennedy grin and said, "Grab it by the legs and listen up."

Which, needless to say, I did. And later, much later, long after Bobby's ascension (more about that anon), I sat down to write his account, incorporating, in the process, the oral histories that had been provided to me by Bobby's closest moving-man associates: Mitchell Bromberg, "Special" Ed Granack, and "Full-Time" John Trefethen. Providentially, my interviews with these invaluable sources were by and large completed at the time of my dismissal from Jake Fuller's employ, a most embarrassing occurrence precipitated by Jake's discovery that someone whose handwriting was identical to my own had been padding the hours on my time card. And, strange though it may seem, my termination coincided, *to the day*, with the issuance, by the local constabulary, of an arrest warrant in my name. The charge, I presumed, was for one count of burglary in the first degree, although, once apprised of the warrant's existence, I neglected to inquire about the fine print. Indeed, under the circumstances, I deemed it prudent to relocate with alacrity. Hence, my current domicile in Kalispell.

I do not tell you this to garner sympathy. After all, why should you or anyone care if I was mistakenly identified by the owners of the rococo mansion? No doubt you have sufficient troubles of your own. Still, it was owing to *my* troubles—and to my resultant abrupt departure from Seattle—that I was unable to conduct a final series of interviews with my furniture-moving colleagues. These interviews—had they transpired—would have shed light on the few remaining opaque intervals in the postmortem annals of Bobby Kennedy. But since the interviews did not take place, those intervals remained opaque, a state of affairs that, from the standpoint of literary aesthetics, simply would not do.

Thus, the discerning reader may note one or more instances of truly inconsequential conjecture—mere trifles, barely visible dabs of purely fictitious linguistical putty—reluctantly inserted by this humble author to plug up small gaps in the chronology that follows.

The reader will also note that in the interests of authenticity—and at no small sacrifice to my vanity—I have locked my thesaurus in a drawer. Yes, I have done my best, throughout the ensuing text, to relate Bobby's tale as I heard it from others: in the everyday, un-adorned, and all-too-often crude vernacular utilized by moving men, ex-convicts, and hardboiled, if Harvard-educated, politicians.

S.V.H.
Kalispell, Montana
February 1991

ONE

Not all prison guards are terrible. Some are kind. Some try to be helpful. A few even have a sense of humor.

Still, many prison guards are terrible. Many of them are coarse, vulgar churls who really enjoy making other people suffer. Especially cons on the wrong side of the mob, which is to say sorry bastards like Bobby Kennedy.

Not that anyone knew that the guy who went down for the attempted murder of Carlos Marcello was, in fact, the reincarnated Bobby. They just thought he was an out-of-work moving man.

And maybe that was the problem, come to think of it. Not the moving man part but the out-of-work part. You know how it goes when you're unemployed. All that time on your hands to get wrapped up in yourself. To magnify grudges. To go off the deep end.

Which is not to condone Bobby's crime. I'm merely suggesting that he had some real gripes. Take what happened when he died just for starters. The way they handled his case in the afterworld. The countless delays.

The surly clerks. The lost files. The incompetent lawyers and judges. It was worse, Bobby claimed, than CIA under Dulles.

A harsh assessment, to be sure. But who can blame him? After dragging things out for nineteen years, the ruling was that there wasn't a ruling! They couldn't figure out if he was good or he was bad, if he merited entrance to Heaven. So what did they do in their infinite wisdom? They returned him to earth. As an adult! With total recall of his previous life.

They wanted to test Bobby's mettle. They wanted to see how he'd handle himself. They *recycled* the guy.

Just absurd.

And then there was the matter of Bobby's powers. Sure, it's nice when the gods give you magic. But it's kind of a two-edged sword. At least when it comes with caveats. All those rules and regulations were a pain. He was not permitted, for example, to manufacture money, even if he was starving and on the streets. And he couldn't use his magic to influence elections, even if a Democrat was threatened. Even if a Democrat with sterling credentials was just a nudge away from victory at the polls.

He couldn't visit his kids. He couldn't visit his

grandkids. He couldn't use his powers to win the lottery. Hell, there was actually an ordinance prohibiting harassment of that pissant, Eugene McCarthy.

Bobby hated Eugene McCarthy. And I guess I would've, too, if I were him. At least after that scene in the hospital. This was back in Life One, in California. And there was Bobby Kennedy with a brain full of bullets, with his head swollen up to twice its size. His wife was there, his children were there, he was forty-two years old, and he was dying. Dying, and with him the national soul. Or at least a percentage of it.

Not the moment for McCarthy to appear. But he did, he showed up at the hospital. Ostensibly to pay his respects. And what do you think that effete bastard said to the grief-stricken throng in the corridor? He said, "Let's get together and unite behind Lyndon."

Talk about a no-class act.

Which perhaps explains why, when they sent Bobby back, the gods covered their asses on McCarthy. But what *could* Bobby do with his magic? He did fine by the movers, for one thing. Or so I heard from Special Ed and Full-Time John. According to them, and to Mitchell, as well, he was a vigilant, effective wonder worker. The type who was constantly shrinking large cabinets to make them fit into undersized elevators. Who never failed, if a weak or clumsy partner lost his grip, to stand there and magically hold up both ends of an eight-foot-long loaded credenza. He was fiercely devoted to easing the lives of his fellow moving men.

It was a worthy endeavor. And no doubt gratifying. But what about his life beyond the trucks? Where was his soul after work?

I strongly suspect that's the key to his crime. Bobby's pent-up frustration, I mean. Like when he tried to come to terms with his issues. When he read all those books about his family. Night after night, seven nights of the week, holed up alone in the rooming house. Devouring tomes on the Kennedy clan. Steeping himself in its dark side.

Not that the authors always got the straight scoop. On certain matters, in fact, they never did. For example, the statistics on Jack's women. Every author had to take a stab at that. And every author claimed to have the final word. Yet the estimates ranged from a low of thirteen to a high of thirty-two White House trysts. And as Bobby well knew, based on memos from Edgar Hoover, the actual figure was much closer to fifty-nine!

Bobby sure got a chuckle out of that. But mostly there was nothing to laugh about. For, statistics aside, the broad charges rang true. You know what I mean: the bad parenting. The incessant demands to win at all costs. The morally hollow role models. And you don't have to be a certified shrink to figure out where this research would lead. Predictably, inevitably, as Bobby checked out his past—plus the sleazy goings-on while he'd been dead—he had negative thoughts about Daddy. And he was feeling pretty hostile towards Mother. And at Teddy, the fuck-up. At his kids. At the world.

But the gods wouldn't let him make contact. He had no place to go with his rage. Oh, he sent off some letters, if you could call the things letters. They were more like wrathful screeds about betrayal. A jumble of barely coherent angry wails in which he asked for affirmation of his feelings. Along with any cash that could be spared. A hundred dollars would do. Even fifty. He was strapped, he explained, and he would be 'til payday.

He sent a letter to his big sister, Eunice. He sent another, marked "personal," to Teddy's office. And when the letters came back because the postage fell off, Bobby made several late-night calls. From the phone booth across from the rooming house. He tried reaching Ethel at Hickory Hill. He tried his old school chum, David Hackett. He tried ex-Harvard roommates. He tried anyone he knew. All he wanted was to hear a friendly voice. That, and to get a few things off his chest, such as his views on why Dukakis was a lousy candidate. But each time he dialed, the phone line went dead.

Next, he considered a visit. A sneak weekend trip to Hyannis. But such trips were against regulations. Besides, the cost of flying was prohibitive. And the instant he *thought* about flying by magic, the Gods intervened with a migraine.

It was hard to be thwarted like that. Especially hard for a fellow like Bobby, a fellow who was used to bending rules. Who broke rules with impunity as a matter of course.

Until he got killed, that is.

Which brings to mind another irony, a galling irony. I mean as bad as Bobby was about breaking the rules, his sins were no match for brother Jack's.

Yet Jack, being Jack, charmed his way past The Keepers. Slipped in, as if Valhalla was a chippy. As if entering Heaven was no more of a challenge than getting into some pretty blonde's pants.

But don't get me going on that! The point isn't Jack and his floozies. The point is that Bobby suffered many rebuffs long *before* he was sent to the joint.

Take Loretta, who worked at the book store. The used

book store at Fourteenth and Pine. The one Bobby went to because, in the back, it had a whole section on Kennedys.

Well, she caught Bobby's fancy, Loretta did. Caught it big time, in fact. He was smitten. And notwithstanding his two-decade layoff from romance, the puppy-love stage went well. But then, the early phase always does.

You know, the flirting that took place at the register. The smiles, the idle chitchat about the titles. The way she'd remark that he looked like a Kennedy. Or agree with his opinion that it wasn't Sirhan. That there was no way in hell he could've fired nine shots from a gun with six chambers. *No way.* So it must've been Cesar, the security guard, who shot Bobby, point blank, in the head.

Not to mention those moments when Loretta bent down to bag up his Kennedy books. Giving Bobby a chance to appraise her fine hips. The slope of her breasts. The whole effect.

Well, that stage went nicely, as I say. As did the first several dates. And the first kiss.

But according to Mitch, the gods set Bobby up with their hands-off approach to this relationship. And there's much to be said for Mitch's theory.

I don't mean to imply that the gods egged Bobby on, that they urged him to pull foolish stunts. Such as telling Loretta who he actually was (which he was not allowed to do except with moving men). Or attempting to charm or impress or delude or intensify her sex drive with his magic. Again, that was strictly *verboten*. And Bobby adhered to the rules.

But even the gods can't change history. And the sad fact remains that Bobby's death occurred just before the women's movement caught on. Yet when he came back to earth he received no advice. Not a squib of information was proffered. Not so much as a cursory two-minute briefing on basic post-feminist mores.

In short, as Mitch said, the gods set Bobby up for the disaster that struck on date five. It took place at the Woodland Park Zoo. And as you've probably guessed, it was a long-peckered zebra that set the debacle in motion.

Loretta giggled at the sight. Bobby laughed. And made what he thought was an innocuous remark about a movie called "Long Dong Silver." Which his moving man buddy, Special Ed, had gone to see, and had reenacted for the guys on Monday morning.

It was the typical morning scene: Bobby and John were loading the trucks with clean, padded blankets and four-wheeled dollies. Mitchell was checking out the color-coded tool kits to make sure all the tools were accounted for. Jimmy and Mike and some part-time guys were standing around sipping coffee, while Ed was goofing off, doing bits from "Long Dong."

Which Bobby mentioned to Loretta. As an aside. He said the zebra reminded him of Special Ed's antics.

"This was some pornographic film?" Loretta said.

"I guess," Bobby said.

They were passing the hippos.

"That fellow sounds Asian to me. *Long Dong,*" Bobby said. "Southeast Asian first name. Jewish last name. Solid ethnic. In the bag!"

"What?" said Loretta.

"Just thinking out loud."

"About what?"

"Past elections."

"Are you nuts?"

Bobby nervously ran his hand through his hair, the way he used to when he had to give a speech. He hadn't meant to slip into Life One. And something else was amiss, he wasn't sure what. So he tried to finesse the problem. By employing the charm, the old Kennedy charm, the humility portion of the charm. "I sure *hope* I'm not nuts," he said. "But I do get confused at my age."

He flashed the Kennedy grin. He winked a Kennedy wink. He was giving it his best.

But it didn't take. Loretta was immune to the tired ploys. "*I'll* say you're confused," she said.

Then she lit into Bobby. Full force. Regarding all sorts of things he'd never heard of before. E.g., objectification of women. And a language that was riddled with misogynist terms. And glass ceilings in the workplace. And dead white males. "Goddamn dead, goddamn white, goddamn males," she said.

Bobby was surprised by her tirade. Puzzled and alarmed by certain aspects. He said, "What have you got against dead white males?"

"That they're not dead enough," Loretta said.

"Just my luck," Bobby said.

"What does *that* mean?" she said.

"Oh, nothing," Bobby said. "But I don't understand—"

"So I gathered."

"Why you got so upset about a movie," he said. "I mean there *is* a First Amendment in this country."

"Jesus Christ," said Loretta. "You're a fucking troglodyte."

"That's unladylike language," Bobby said.

"I don't fucking believe this."

"Me neither," he said.

"No wonder you read about Kennedys. Those people *hate* women."

They passed the giraffes.

"Those people *killed* Marilyn Monroe. They fucked her and killed her."

Bobby visibly flinched.

She had struck a raw nerve.

This wasn't funny.

Nor, for that matter, was the spat that ensued: the charges, the countercharges, the cheap shots. And there's no need to recount every thrust, every jab, every nasty little shiv and innuendo.

Suffice it to say that by the time they had reached the pride and joy of the zoo—the new elephant house—Bobby Kennedy had accused Loretta of fraud. Of harboring low-brow tastes. Of working in a book store to mask the shameful fact that she'd acquired all her knowledge from reading tabloids.

And she'd accused him of his own kind of fraud. Of pretending to be a sensitive man when, in fact, he was a porno-loving churl.

"That's completely untrue," Bobby said. "I didn't

even *see* the goddamned movie. I'm the *prude* of my family. I'm the moral high ground. I'm—"

"Full of shit," said Loretta. "And perverted. A lecher, no doubt, in a long line of lechers. I can't *believe* I was attracted to you!"

"Same here!" Bobby said.

"Witch burner!" she said.

"Witch burner?"

"You heard me," Loretta said.

They were both steaming mad. And it got worse. When they passed the barnyard animal exhibit, Bobby pointed to a mud-splattered pig. "See the snout on that thing?" he said. "That's you in a goddamn nutshell. You look down your snout at us blue-collar guys. You think that you're better than us."

To which Loretta replied—at the reptile house—that he had a lot in common with the salamanders.

"How so?" Bobby said.

"Potential," she said. "For having your conscious-ness raised."

"I see," Bobby said.

"No you don't," said Loretta. "That's the point. You don't see. You're a clod."

"Well, speaking of seeing, see that ape over there?"

"Over where?"

"Over there," Bobby said. "The one with the baby."

"What about her?" said Loretta.

"She doesn't shave under her arms."

"So?" said Loretta.

"She's an *ape*," Bobby said. "She doesn't have access to razors. But what I'd like to know is what's *your* excuse?"

Well, this was too much for Loretta. The last straw, so to speak. She slapped Bobby! Smacked him right in the kisser.

And stalked off.

Leaving Bobby to stand there and rub his sore mouth in a crowd made up largely of children.

Bobby gave a brave smile to one scared little boy.

The little boy burst out crying.

Others joined him.

While the parents looked stern as they gazed at this man, at this screwball with the bloody lower lip. Who appeared to be confused. Who *was* confused. Because he didn't know the score, didn't have the faintest clue, about the modern views on armpit hair and women.

But ignorant or not, he couldn't stand there forever. So, still rubbing his face, he started home. Bobby walked the whole way to save on bus fare. And the longer he walked, the madder he got. Witch burner indeed, Bobby thought. Descendant of lechers, indeed! I mean even if his daddy *was* a horny old goat, who the hell was she to say so? Who indeed?

Not to mention that business about Marilyn Monroe. The whole *world* thought he killed her.

It wasn't fair.

Shit, Bobby muttered. *Goddamncocksuckerpiss.*

He was cussing like the moving man he was.

But he was thinking like the Kennedy he was. And that was the bad part, the Kennedy part. The part that couldn't, simply couldn't, accept defeat.

Which pretty much explains how Bobby landed in the joint. Or at least the route he took.

It was direct.

Step One was to piss off the gods. To piss them off royally, in fact. To make them so mad that they shut off his magic.

The way he went about it was familiar. Nauseatingly familiar for those who knew him. Which is to say, he chose to bypass formal channels. Just as he and Jack had done back in the sixties. When they circumvented State because of people like Adlai, because of all those striped-pants sissies who made life difficult.

Their solution was the rogue operation. E.g., the plot to kill Fidel Castro. Or, failing that, to cause his beard to fall out by lacing his cigars with hair remover.

Check it out if you don't believe me. Head on down to your local library. Or to the Kennedy section of Loretta Easton's store. It's right there in the history books. Under "Operation Mongoose."

Which Bobby ran. Sounds preposterous, I know, but it's the truth. He was the unofficial head; he was the President's man. He was the *author* of that scatterbrained scheme.

And to make matters worse, the original plan called for hiring expert hit men from the mob. Yes, you heard me correctly: the mob. The same bunch of thugs who Bobby Kennedy was pursuing, who he was using his high office to destroy.

In short, it was a downright bozo move. A move that put all sorts of loonies in cahoots. Loonies like Jimmy Hoffa, for example. And the boss of New Orleans—the boss of all bosses—Don Carlos Marcello himself. And ring-sporting gangsters like that fellow Jack Ruby. And CIA types like Howard Hunt. Plus Sam Giancana, David Ferrie, and others.

It was quite the collection of sociopaths; the best and brightest sick minds in America. And they all reached the same conclusion: that Fidel Castro's beard was not a serious threat to business. But the Kennedy brothers were. So if they cut off the head, which is to say, Jack, they could stop the Bobby tail from fucking wagging.

Well that's what happens when you bypass formal channels. Assassinations in Dallas. Shit like that.

You would've thought he'd learned his lesson in Life One. But here he was in Life Two, repeating history. Electing to avoid the everyday route. And electing, in the process, to not act civil.

By civil, I mean civil. As in civil. Like showing up at the book store—that would be civil. And maybe bringing flowers and looking sheepish. Maybe saying he was sorry for blowing his stack. And admitting to Loretta that he was lonely. Maybe even admitting that he might've been wrong. And then requesting, in good faith, to hear her out. And then listening, politely, as she spoke. And then stating his views in a moderate tone. Being gracious as he talked about the First Amendment. Acknowledging the dangers of free speech run amok, while expressing concern for the Bill of Rights.

There really isn't much to it—acting civil. And he really did have that option available. He could've tried, at any rate. It might've worked. And then again, he might've fallen on his face. She could've told him to scram or she'd call the police.

But them's the breaks, as they say. Love is risky. Besides, this whole debate is academic. He didn't go to the store, he didn't try to be nice, he didn't bring her fresh flowers after work.

Instead, he tried to brainwash Loretta. He tried to do it from a distance with his powers. He tried to get her to think he was right on all counts; that Long Dong Silver was a frivolous issue; that the charges she'd leveled were entirely baseless, especially any charges involving Marilyn.

It was a flagrant violation of regulations. It reeked of Kennedy hubris. And it was lazy. It insulted the gods. It was a brazen affront.

So the gods came down hard, very hard. They did what Jack did to those Bay of Pigs guys: they cut Bobby off cold in mid-battle.

This occurred at two o'clock on Monday morning, as Bobby lay on his bed in the rooming house. He was about to lock into his ex-girlfriend's soul—to enter her mind surreptitiously—when Bobby felt it, a sudden loss of vitality. A sudden loss of the tingles, the music, the voice, the colored spirals and all those side effects of magic.

Bobby didn't panic at first. He knew the magic would return. It always did. This was just a power outage, so to speak. A minor glitch, an inconvenience, a tiny setback, nothing more. It was *bound* to return.

Except it didn't. Not that day at work or the day after that. Or the week or the month after that. He couldn't levitate pianos or couches or desks. Hell, he couldn't even lift a fucking pencil! Unless he chose to do it the regular way.

He wasn't special anymore. He wasn't anything. He was just another Joe who clocked in and clocked out, a development that raises questions about the gods. I mean why was their response so draconian? Why, in the past, had the gods been content to merely intervene in sticky matters? To simply thwart Bobby, to keep him in bounds, by making postage fall off, for example. Or making phone lines go dead. Or doling out migraines. To be sure, the headaches hurt. But they were temporary.

So why, in this case, did they get so incensed that they shut off his magic indefinitely? Why didn't they give him a warning? Just tell the poor bastard to get a grip on himself, to straighten up and fly right, to hold his water?

The answer, if you'll excuse me, is who the fuck knows? Gods are gods, after all. They make the rules.

Well, be that as it may, he'd completed Step One of his aforementioned trip to the slammer. Step One, you may recall, was to provoke the Higher Powers by acting like a complete jerk.

Step Two was to get himself fired. And oddly enough, Step Two was much harder, since it required more than one bonehead move. It required—catch this—a whole string of dumb moves *plus* a vicious assault on a chair.

Yes, it really took some doing to get fired. It often does if you're a valued employee. Not that Jake knew about the magical stuff, and not that Bobby needed it to shine. He was strong for his size, he didn't drink on the job, he was polite to the clients, he earned his keep. In fact he earned it and then some. He was profitable.

So Jake was inclined to bend over backward when Bobby started acting erratically. When he started pulling stunts like showing up late, or babbling about sinister cover-ups. About how unfair it was that *everyone* knew that Lee Harvey Oswald was a patsy. That a cabal led by Carlos Marcello himself took JFK out in mob style. You know that style—the three-gunmen approach. The tri-angular-fire approach. The mob's can't-miss-solution-to-any-problem approach.

Well, everyone knew about that. But no one gave a hoot about JFK's brother, about the fact that evil forces took *him* out. And that *both* hits were ordered by Carlos Marcello. And that the prick who did the brother was still at large.

It's all Bobby talked about at work. On the dock, in the trucks, over beers with the guys. He had bullets on the brain, so to speak. Conflicting reports about who shot who when, impossible trajectories, and powder burns. Documents ignored by the Warren Commission. Ignored or even altered by the CIA. And the usual stuff about missing body parts, inept county coroners, all of that.

Initially, Jake couldn't believe it. His most reliable driver, his steadiest man, had become a conspiracy nut. And that's not the worst Jake put up with. There were sloppy work habits in abundance. Like not properly folding the furniture pads, but simply tossing them haphazardly in the truck. Thereby creating an unprofessional look, the kiss of death in a word-of-mouth business. Or not tying loads down securely enough, the surest method for inviting damage claims. Or Bobby's irritating practice of leaving handtrucks and dollies strewn here and there on the freight dock, instead of stacking them neatly as he had in the past.

He had an attitude problem, all right. A very serious problem, in fact. And I haven't even mentioned his newfound disregard for putting tools back where they came from. You would've thought ratchet sockets grew on trees!

But as implied, Bobby's boss took the long view. If a guy was good once, he could be good again. So Jake cut Bobby slack, a lot of slack. Maybe, in retrospect, a bit too much slack.

Whatever the case, Jake had limits. And they made themselves known in the form of a call that Jake received from a customer one afternoon. This customer, a lawyer at a big downtown firm, was having a conniption fit. It seems that one of the workers who'd come to drop of the chair, the restored Chippendale for the reception area, had opted for dismemberment over delivery. And he'd performed the vile deed in front of terrified clients and a terrified staff in the outer lobby. "He smashed the teak frame!" said the lawyer. "The fellow smashed it to bits with his hammer." And then, said the lawyer, he used his long-handled screwdriver to gouge the authentic upholstery. "He just punctured those cushions. It was *savage!*"

And that wasn't all the scoundrel did. When he finished assaulting the innocent chair, he delivered a passionate speech. A harangue about misguided priorities. Standing right there amidst the havoc he'd wreaked, ankle deep in expensive chair stuffing, he proceeded to jab his index finger at the air. "Five grand for a chair!" he said. "Five grand for a chair for rich fatsoes!" he said. He chopped the air with his hand. "Five grand!"

Then he talked about some ways to spend five grand. About the thousands of shoes the same money could buy for disadvantaged children in the ghettos. About the lifesaving medicines the money could buy for all those widows on fixed incomes who ate catfood. About regressive tax structures, about the need to do more, about America's ability to do better.

At which point, said the lawyer, the diatribe ceased, and Bobby cleaned up the mess and left.

"Just cleaned up and left?" Jake said.

"Well," said the lawyer, "that other fellow who was with him—I believe Mitch was his name—he apologized. He said your man was having personal problems. Had a tiff with his girlfriend or something like that."

Jake sighed. "So that's it."

"Who is he?"

"He's no one," Jake said. "He's an ex-employee. I'll fire his ass when he gets here."

Which is not to imply that Jake lacked for insurance. If anything, he was prudent to a fault. In addition to the usual—accidents, floods, liability, theft and the lot—he was covered for volcanic eruptions. And for conventional and nuclear war. And for business interruptions due to economic downturns or the effects of a post-earthquake tsunami. And for looting resulting from civil unrest.

The man shelled out bucks for insurance.

But that only made matters worse. Because with all that he spent every month on the stuff, he still had to pay for Bobby's outburst. "Five grand out of pocket!" Jake said. "Five fucking big ones!" he shouted at Bobby when he and Mitch returned to the shop. "Five thousand smackers! And for what? A dumb speech with *unmistakable* communist overtones!"

Jake was bent out of shape, and who could blame him? No insurance on earth pays for bleeding heart sentiments that are expressed by busting up an antique chair.

So that took care of Step Two: getting fired. And the jump to Step Three—to committing a crime that resulted in a trip to the hoosegow—was, relatively speaking, a breeze. I mean there was Bobby Kennedy with time on his hands, lots of time to nurse grudges, to stew. To dwell on how rotten and unfair his life was. And to find an appropriate scapegoat.

Who, as you've probably guessed, was Marcello. Not that there weren't other eligible candidates, highly qualified objects of blame. Such as J. Edgar Hoover, for example. And Daddy and Mother and Reagan's trickle-down theory. And long-peckered zebras. And God. And land wars in Asia. And overpriced chairs. And his big brother's hormones.

To name a few.

Still, no goat could hold a candle to Marcello. I mean if it weren't for Marcello, Jack wouldn't be dead, which would've spared the crushing grief of '63. And Bobby's own bloody end in '68. And his painful rebirth and being lonely and broke as he lay on his bed in Life Two. As he lay there and realized that he, Bobby Kennedy, would soon be applying for food stamps.

It was a very depressing prospect. So depressing, so noxious, so completely degrading, that for once this man of action couldn't act. He just stared at the crack in the ceiling. He just lay on his bed for days. In fact, he stared for so long that he had a strange vision: he saw the crack become a runway at Sea-Tac Airport. He saw a plane from New Orleans make a landing. He saw a very old man who was surrounded by thugs, who looked like Carlos Marcello, disembark.

Well, Bobby did what any standard crazy person would do: he took the vision as a sign from above. And he responded with a series of not inconsistent, if arguably wackadoo, moves. To wit, he went to a pawnshop and purchased a gun, rode a bus to the airport, and bought a paper. He unfolded the paper and started reading. Or tried to look like he was reading, at any rate. And when, at long last, his aged nemesis appeared, Bobby whipped out his pistol and fired.

TWO

It made the evening news, Bobby's crime. And of course it's all they talked about at work. Bobby this, Bobby that. It went on for a week.

And then the hoopla died down; the memory faded. Life had to go on; furniture had to be moved. "The guy's a flake and that's that," is how Jake put it.

Still, as Mitchell points out, the whole tawdry affair raises a number of questions about the gods. Fundamental questions about accountability. Difficult questions regarding ethical vacuums. Sobering questions about their judgment. About the visions they show, the information they reveal, to their emotionally marginal charges. I mean they could've aired cartoons on Bobby's ceiling. Or a Rin Tin Tin film. Or nothing at all. *Anything* besides Marcello's whereabouts.

But enough about those cynical bastards. Enough about their cruel and vengeful ways! The point is, down here, if you fuck with the mob, and the mob doesn't kill you right away, and you don't have the money to grease the right palms, you get sent up for a long, long time.

So it was that Bobby Kennedy went to prison. Not that his keepers or fellow convicts were aware of his formidable government resume. As I say, in the joint, they just thought of the guy as a murderous, unemployed moving man. Which is what, in his second life, he was. But he was also the first one, the real Bobby Kennedy. I mean they both were the real Bobby Kennedys. It's just that one of them was dead.

But not really.

Does that clarify the issue? Or simply cloud it? It's such a murky arena—visitations, rebirths, past-life karma, doppelgangers and the lot. Besides, who has time for that shit? You go to work, come home, do the wash, pay the rent, change the oil, floss your teeth, *and it's enough*. Why, I'll bet Bobby himself would agree! Because in spite of his tormented, dark Irish side, bouts of anguish never crimped his can-do style. What use would he have for esoteric debates when he was always stalking out of boring meetings? He didn't have time for long-winded sissies. The man liked results. He was pragmatic. He'd be the *first* to point out that the bottom line in all of this was that whichever Bobby he was, he was in the slammer. And things being how they were, he had no magic or Jesus or old Harvard connections to fall back on. Hell, he couldn't even afford a decent attorney.

But to get back to that subject I left long ago, of nasty, brutish, vulgar prison guards: one afternoon, during Free Movement Period, Bobby Kennedy encountered four of them. It was practically winter, the tenth of December, and for no reason except for boredom mixed with sadism and perhaps a tad of latent homosexuality, the four guards decided to perform a body-cavity search.

They pulled Bobby Kennedy into a cold concrete room. They ordered him to let his pants down. They ordered him to let his underpants down. Then, with his pants and underpants draped around his ankles, they made him waddle over to an old wooden table that was stained here and there with dark spots that might have been blood. "Bend over," said the guard named Mr. Foley, but who the convicts referred to as "Gerbil," owing to his remarkably gerbil-like face. Bobby Kennedy bent over the waist-high table.

"Stretch out your arms," said Gerbil.

Bobby Kennedy stretched out his arms. His hands gripped the edge of the table.

One of the guards held down his left wrist and another guard held down his right wrist. A third guard paced back and forth between them, twirling his night-stick and grinning. From the back of the room Bobby heard Gerbil open a jar of Vaseline and stretch on a latex examination glove.

Bobby tried not to think about what was coming next.

"You're gonna love this," said Gerbil as he rammed his finger up Bobby's rectum. He probed this way and that, crudely speculating all the while about what he might be touching inside Bobby's asshole. Was it contraband, a large hemorrhoid, or just a stray piece of shit? The other guards laughed appreciatively.

Bobby Kennedy felt very sad. He thought wistfully about his previous life when he had served in his brother's cabinet and was considered by everyone— from the lowliest meatheads like Gerbil to the envious vice-president of the United States—to be the second most powerful man in the country. He also thought, with typical Kennedy irony, *and Roy Cohn did this for fun?* But he felt much too degraded to smile. Besides, it's physically difficult, if not impossible, to smile when your nose, mouth and chin are mashed into a blood-stained table top.

Gerbil flapped his finger back and forth. He twisted it idly and moved it slowly up and down. Then he made an odd remark. He was pissed off, he said, because he wasn't scheduled to work on Christmas. Since all guards get paid triple time on Christmas regardless of whether they work, the other three guards looked puzzled. So Gerbil explained his irritation. He said he'd miss the opportunity to laugh at the convicts for spending Christmas Day in prison.

Bobby felt sadder than ever. In an effort to not think about what was happening to him, he tried to conjure up some memories from long ago. He went back in time to Jack's White House days, then further back to Jack's first run for Congress, and finally all the way back to the late 1920s when he was just a little boy. He remembered the big mansion in Bronxville with its seventeen rooms and five acres of landscaped grounds. He remembered the maids, he remembered the gardeners, and he remembered how, as a boy of four, he used to sit on the broad front steps every weekday afternoon waiting for Jack to get home from school. Waiting and hoping that his big brother Jack would take him for a walk and tell him tales about knights and dragons.

How he'd loved those walks with Jack. How he'd worshipped and adored his brother! A lot of times when Bobby got that hollow sensation inside, the one that told him he was different from everybody, he'd look up at Jack and Jack would smile at him and maybe throw him a special wink. Charming Jack. Funny Jack. Sometimes Bobby pretended that Jack was his real dad whereas the man he called "Daddy," the stern fellow in the glasses who he could never quite please no matter how hard he tried, wasn't really his dad but a stranger. Or if not exactly a stranger, then just a friend of his mother's—a special friend, to be sure, but not his dad.

Jack was twelve when Bobby was four. Jack wore a tie and went to school. Jack knew all the stories in the world.

Sometimes when he was sitting on the steps and waiting for Jack to get home, Bobby would close his eyes and make a wish. What he'd wish was that he was Jack and Jack was him. He'd squeeze his eyes shut, stand up, and snap his fingers. He'd twirl around and say "Abracadabra." Then he'd sit down to see what had happened. To see if his legs had grown long and his shorts had become pants because he'd turned into Jack and vice versa.

It never happened.

But Bobby kept trying and hoping. Until one afternoon, a chilly day in October, Bobby realized something. He realized they might have changed places. Conceivably his wish *had* come true. But even if it had he'd never know he was Jack because the person on the stairs was him. The person on the stairs would always be Bobby and he would always be the person on the stairs. I mean even if he wasn't, he'd *think* that he was.

It's kind of hard to explain Bobby's logic. But the point is he realized he was stuck with himself and would have to grow up as Bobby, not Jack.

Naturally this made him despondent. He was so despondent, in fact, that instead of waiting any longer he went for a walk without Jack. He meandered here and there with his head hung down, kicking through the red-orange leaves. He thought about what a useless and horrible person he was, and how he couldn't do anything right. For example, he was terrible at catching footballs. Or at least when it mattered, he was terrible.

It was his big brother Joe who had taught him. Joe was the King of all his siblings. Joe was the King, Jack was the Prince, and Kathleen was the glamorous Queen. Or so Bobby liked to think of them.

Well anyway, whenever Joe came home for visits from prep school, he'd spend hours teaching Bobby how to catch. "Soft hands! Soft hands!" Joe would shout.

And the thing is, if Bobby was tossing the football with a person of no significance he'd have the softest hands in the world. Like if he was playing with Ralph the chauffeur's son, he could catch any pass that came his way. Wobbly passes, shoe-string passes, even over-the-shoulder, long-bomb passes.

He was truly amazing for a four-year-old. He had the grace of a six-year-old star. But the problem was, if Joe was around, Bobby would lose the gift. His hands would get stiff and he'd grab much too hard so the football would bounce away.

Worst of all was if his dad came home. Usually, back then, Mr. Kennedy was in Hollywood. He made big movie deals out there. And according to historians, he was also screwing the daylights out of sex-goddess Gloria Swanson.

But Bobby, being not much older than a toddler, didn't know about screwing yet. All he knew was what had happened last weekend. Daddy was home, standing out on the porch, watching Joe toss the football to him. And the strangest thing had happened to Bobby's arms: it was as if they'd become someone else's. He couldn't control them no matter how hard he tried. They were big heavy clunks he couldn't move. Or at best he could lift them as high as his waist, and the ball would bounce off his chest. He dropped *every* pass that Joe threw to him. Even the baby passes.

He had wanted so badly to show off for his dad, to make him see that he'd practiced and was a star. But Daddy walked away in disgust. And Joe was pretty disappointed, too. If only Jack had been there. That might've made things all right. He might've smiled and given Bobby his special wink. But Jack was in bed with a fever that day. Jack was always in bed with fevers.

Bobby shuddered at the memory and kicked more leaves. "I can never catch passes when it matters," he thought. "Also I am ugly. And very stupid."

He had come to the edge of the grounds. He looked at the clouds in the sky. They were dark, low, and menacing clouds. The wind had picked up and leaves swirled around. It looked like a storm. It *was* a storm.

Bobby realized his clothes would get wet. Mother hated wet clothes and muddy shoes. Worse still, it was almost dinnertime. It might even be past dinnertime. And rule number one in the Kennedy house was be on time for dinner OR ELSE. Bobby wasn't sure what OR ELSE entailed because he'd never been late for dinner. But it wasn't OR ELSE that scared him so much; what scared him was the prospect of Daddy's look. If he came late to the table in wet, muddy clothes, Daddy was sure to scowl. And no one could scowl as fiercely as Daddy.

Lightning flashed, thunder rolled, and wind howled. Huge oaks and maples swayed to and fro. Rain fell in buckets. Bobby ran. He ran back to the mansion as fast as he could, hoping he wouldn't be late. Hoping against hope that when he came to the house, no one would be in the dining room. He scampered across the wide front lawn and bounded up the steps to the porch. Then he plowed through the door, the plate-glass door, which happened to be closed at the time.

Once again, Bobby shuddered at the memory. He remembered his scream. He remembered the blood. He remembered how Daddy had held him.

As for Gerbil, he was having lots of fun. Or as they say nowadays on educational TV, he was pursuing his rapture, his bliss. The man loved his work. He was so integrated! He moved his finger up and down and rubbed his crotch against Bobby's thigh. He was aroused and rubbed some more.

Bobby cringed. Then he took a deep breath and returned to the past. He remembered other days in other autumns. There was the day Jack was killed, of course. And the Missiles of October in '62. And way back in the '40's he remembered something else, which was walking home from chapel with Mary Bailey. Pretty Mary. Sparkling Mary. Perfect Mary. She was tall and blonde with violet eyes. She smelled of honey and everything good.

It was Sunday evening at Milton Academy. The air

had turned brisk and autumn sad as Bobby kicked through the red-orange leaves. He hung his head behind the forelock that would someday be famous as he walked behind Mary Bailey. Bobby loved her but was too scared to talk. That's why he followed her four feet behind.

What a gawky adolescent he had been! What a shy and sweet kid. So what had happened? When had he turned so ruthless and mean? What became of that gangly sophomore?

Bobby thought about his life before he'd been killed. He thought about his youth and then he cried. He tried holding it back but he couldn't.

Gerbil removed his finger. He told Bobby to pull up his underpants. Then he told him to pull up his pants. Bobby shuffled to the door with his head hung low so that no one would see his tears. But all the guards saw them anyway.

"Baby!" said Gerbil as he gave Bobby a kick. It was a kick in the shin. It hurt. Bobby hopped around and grabbed at his leg while the guards called him names such as "Faggot." And "Douchebag" and "Pissface" and "Motherfuckingprick." And "Jewlovingnigger–lovingmaggot."

Gerbil kicked him again and Bobby hopped out the door.

"See you later, Scumbag," Gerbil said.

That night in the chow hall Bobby Kennedy sat alone. He stirred his food slowly but didn't eat it. *Thirty years for attempted murder.* Thirty fucking years for botching the hit on the prick who had had Johnny whacked.

"I blew it," Bobby thought as he stirred. It was a classic example of good intentions gone astray, an unforgivable Adlai Stevenson sort of move. Not that there was any failure of nerve. When Bobby hated, Bobby hated, and that was that. But as Carlos Marcello stepped off the plane on his way to a mob meeting in Seattle, Bobby shot him point blank *and didn't kill him!* He didn't even wound the SOB. Or put a burn in the cocksucker's custom-made suit.

The explanation? Bobby's pistol had jammed.

Bobby looked down at the food on his plate. He got a whiff of the stuff: bologna stew. He considered the food as he stirred it some more. "This stew looks like puke," he thought.

The word was out, of course. Everyone knew about Gerbil and Bobby and the body-cavity search. Everyone knows everything in prison. That's why none of the cons bothered Bobby that night by trying to sit with him. Or by asking for favors such as writing their briefs. Bobby was a jailhouse lawyer. He was an excellent jailhouse lawyer. As a former attorney general of the United States of America, he certainly possessed fine credentials. And he never turned down a request for help, even if a case was hopeless. Especially if a case was hopeless.

But tonight he didn't care about his brothers. Not even about his Indian brothers. There were plenty of Natives in the joint. And, racially speaking, they were the lowest of the low, just as they'd been back in '68. They had voted for Bobby that year. They had turned out in droves in South Dakota. So here in the joint he had repaid the favor by helping to get them a sweat lodge. He'd put together a brief in which he'd argued, quite eloquently, for freedom of religious expression. And lo and behold, the judge who read the brief had handed down a favorable ruling. So the Native Americans had gotten their lodge, much to the consternation of the warden.

The warden loathed Bobby, and feared him. But his Indian friends had told Bobby Kennedy he was the only white con they could trust. In the past this had made Bobby proud. Tonight, however, he thought "Big fucking deal." His shin and butt hurt. He hated life.

What if Jimmy Hoffa or Roy Cohn could see him now? That would be the last straw, Bobby thought. But Jimmy and Roy were dead and gone, as were Hubert and Lyndon and all his enemies. And Daddy and Jack and Joe and Kathleen.

Everyone's dead, Bobby thought.

Bobby shivered. It was cold in the chow hall. He heard shouting across the room. There was some kind of argument taking place. But for once he didn't try to break it up. For once he didn't try to smooth things over. What did he care? He'd just follow the code—the code of convict survival—*don't get involved.*

Bobby listlessly stirred his bologna stew and remembered Jack's words on obligation: "To those whom much is given, much is required," Jack used to say.

"Fuck that shit," Bobby thought.

He tried not to think about what had happened that day, about Gerbil's pig eyes and probing finger. But naturally, by trying not to think about it, that's all he could think about.

The shouting by the east door grew louder. Suddenly, Bobby heard Noodle's voice. Noodle, who had put both his children through college by robbing banks and an occasional armored car, was Bobby's best friend in the joint. He was an excellent mimic and a fine raconteur who could play a mean banjo when the spirit moved him. No matter how depressed Bobby Kennedy got about his life and death and resurrection and so forth, Noodle could make Bobby laugh. Noodle knew how to make everyone laugh, which is a rare and precious gift for men in prison.

Bobby looked across the room at Noodle. He was arguing with Gerbil, of all people. Now Bobby really paid attention. He saw Gerbil, fat Gerbil, with his fat fucking face, standing by the open east door. Outside it was dark, a raw and wet Northwest night. Gerbil twirled his nightstick while Noodle gestured. Noodle said something and Gerbil shook his head "No."

Bobby shivered in the draft. He understood. Gerbil was refusing to shut the door and Noodle was insisting that he do it. Noodle was right, of course. The convicts were cold and it's against regulations to make them be cold for no reason. But to challenge a guard is a major infraction that can earn you thirty days in the hole.

Bobby had never been to the hole but he'd heard all about it from Noodle. About the shit on the walls and the mold and the rats. Noodle often went to the hole. For giving guards lip. For attempting escapes. For strutting around like a rooster.

Bobby remembered his first days in prison. It was Noodle who'd saved him from his ignorance. For no reason except kindness Noodle took him aside and gave him an education. He'd told Bobby which guards were just regular Joes and which ones were perverts and sadists. And how to keep his eyes low and walk like a slave so as not to provoke the mean guards. And which convicts would rape him in a minute if they could, and the best ways to steer clear of such bulldogs. He'd cited the snitches and the child molesters: to talk to them could mean death.

Good old Noodle.

Gerbil took a step and raised his nightstick. He was slowly advancing on Noodle. And so were the guards from the other sides of the room. They had no-nonsense looks. Things got quiet.

Bobby thought about a day when Noodle made him laugh by telling a ridiculous story. It was about feeding an Alka-Seltzer to his favorite pet chicken because the chicken couldn't keep her food down. But instead of getting better, Henny Penny exploded.

"That's awful," Bobby said as he laughed.

"I know," Noodle said. "There were drumsticks all over."

Bobby laughed until he cried.

Good old Noodle.

Gerbil and the others were drawing closer to his friend. Bobby stopped stirring his food. He put down his spoon and stood up. Then he walked across the room to the open east door. He slammed the door shut and stared at Gerbil.

Now things got really super-quiet.

Gerbil and the guards weren't sure what to do. Should they go after Noodle or Bobby? So Bobby helped them make up their minds. He walked up to Gerbil. "Hi, Scumbag," he said. Then he spat a big gob in Gerbil's face.

The guards beat up Bobby with their clubs. They did it in a highly professional manner, just as they'd learned in guard school. The recipient of the beating was screaming in pain and bleeding from head to toe. Yet not one single bone was broken! When Bobby finally fainted they clubbed him some more. Then they threw him in the hole and locked the door.

Bobby wasn't lonely at first. Or hungry or frightened or anything else. All he was was full of pain, unadulterated pain, and all he did was writhe and moan and puke and so forth. After a few days, however, he began to recover and to carefully examine his new home. It looked a lot like in the movies, only worse. I mean a rat on the screen and a rat in a cell are two different matters altogether. And ditto for the rusty steel cot with no mattress, and the bucket in the corner for human waste.

It stank in the hole. It was cold in the hole. Bobby huddled in a corner and shivered. He was running a fever and he was all black and blue. He stared at a lightbulb on the ceiling. It was covered with mesh and it never went off. There was also a TV camera. It was bolted in near the top of the south wall. It enabled the guards to watch Bobby all day, but there was no one for Bobby to watch: there weren't any windows in the concrete cell, and the door was made of reinforced steel.

The formal name, by the way, for this punishment cell was the Intensive Management Unit. Or IMU for short. Thus it sounded like an in-house consulting division and not a hole for rats and men that smelled like shit.

But getting back to that reinforced door: there was a slot in the middle for sliding trays of food in, and the guard who did the sliding was usually Gerbil. He liked to stand outside and say "I'm spitting in your food." Or for a change he'd say "I'm pissing in your food." Then he'd slide the tray in and take the old tray back.

Bobby's feeding was a once-a-day routine. And every three days a phalanx of guards would come in to change Bobby's slop bucket. They'd always club him a little in a friendly sort of way, just enough to make him writhe and scream a bit.

Needless to say, Bobby didn't eat his food, what with

the garnish made of Gerbil's spit and piss. So Bobby grew thinner and weaker by the day, and eventually he began to hallucinate.

The first person he saw was Tip O'Neill. Not Tip the fat Speaker who stood up to Ronald Reagan, but Tip the young glad-handing voluble pol who Bobby assumed was a hack. Actually Tip O'Neill was never a hack, but it was easy to mistake him for one: he had a red bulbous nose and a lower-class accent.

Bobby never liked the old hacks. Jack found them amusing and they liked him in turn. They loved Jack, in fact, as did everyone.

But the ruthless young Bobby had viewed them with scorn and treated them disrespectfully. Like that time up in Boston when Jack first ran for the Senate and some hacks were hanging out at the office. They were shooting the breeze (which is their major occupation) while the volunteers around them were hard at work.

Well, this got on Bobby's nerves and made him angry. There were hundreds and hundreds of envelopes to lick, and stamps to be placed on the envelopes. There were thousands of phone calls that had to be made, and doors to be knocked on throughout the districts. And here were these hacks just standing around. So Bobby did the unthinkable: he kicked them out! "You work or you leave," he told the old men.

They couldn't believe their ears. Who was this arrogant punk? It'll lead to no good, they assured each other. He'll get his comeuppance and get it soon. His brother will lose the election, they said, and things will return to normal.

But Jack survived the Eisenhower tide, and a mere eight years later he was President.

Bobby hunched in a corner and stared at Tip. He remembered another incident. It was back in the summer of '56. There were rumors afloat that Adlai Stevenson was considering Jack for vice-president. So Bobby asked Tip to get him a seat on the floor at the National Convention. "It's imperative that you do this," said Bobby to Tip. "I need to control our people."

Well, Tip asked all the delegates he knew if they'd give up their seats for Bobby. But when no one said yes, Tip did it himself: he gave his credentials to Bobby. To say the least, this was a generous gesture. It is almost unheard of for a member of Congress to give up a seat at the convention.

But did Bobby thank Tip? No, he didn't. Not one simple call was forthcoming. Not even a two-line note. Understandably, Tip became furious. He was so mad, in fact, that he called up old Joe to tell him his son was an ingrate. And old Joe replied that Bobby was spoiled, a hard worker to be sure, but also spoiled.

Not that Bobby cared at the time. In his opinion, back then, mere peons like Tip were *supposed* to grant him favors when he asked. What did he care about Tip O'Neill's feelings, or the feelings of some useless old hacks? The fact is he didn't even know they had feelings.

Now things were different, of course. Now he, Bobby Kennedy, was the convict, the scum. Now he was the one without power.

He looked up at Tip and said, "I'm sorry." But Tip wasn't there; he had faded away.

Bobby shivered and felt ashamed of himself. The cold concrete dug into his back. He was dizzy and filled with self-loathing. And as usually happens when one is filled with self-loathing, he went into the old downward spiral. Bobby started to remember all the odious things he had done in his previous life. Like that time, in '61, when he humiliated Chester Bowles—that shameless admirer of Adlai's—by literally poking the old fellow in the gut while chewing his sissified ass. He had done the poking number at a cabinet meeting. Even McNamara called the outburst ruthless.

And what was poor Chester's offense? Just this: he'd been right all along. Yes, he'd had the temerity to oppose the Bay of Pigs, and to note his opposition when the invasion failed. "You mean you *used* to be against it!" Bobby raved as he poked. "As of now you were all for it! From the start!"

Not to mention the six months Bobby spent working as assistant counsel to that notorious liar and bully, Senator Joseph McCarthy. Or the times he called Gore Vidal and a limousine driver a fag and a fatso, respectively.

Thinking back on what a pugnacious little snot he used to be, Bobby had to admit that Hubert Humphrey may have been justified when, in the aftermath of the bitter 1960 West Virginia primary fight, he made reference to "that spoiled young juvenile, Bobby." And, in retrospect, perhaps it hadn't been terribly judicious of Bobby to respond by telling reporters, "My first job, after getting my brother elected President, will be the political destruction of Hubert Humphrey."

Bobby stared at the light bulb that never went off. Then he remembered something even more embarrassing. It was a magazine-selling business he had started in order to supplement his allowance back when he was growing up in Bronxville. He signed up a lot of customers but soon got bored with the time-consuming hand-delivery aspect of the operation. And so, as Kennedyhating journalist Victor Lasky has meticulously documented, little Bobby "took to covering his route with magazines stacked in the back of the family's chauffeur-driven Rolls Royce."

Bobby winced at the thought of what Noodle would say if he knew of his rich-kid past. Or worse still, what if his old moving-man buddy, the tart-tongued Special Ed, had gotten hold of Lasky's book, *Robert F. Kennedy: the Myth and the Man*? It could've happened if Ed had gone to Loretta's store. If he had gone there and asked for a Kennedy book, she might well have recommended it out of spite. And what if, God forbid, Ed had read about the way the Kennedy children were in the habit of "stepping from their boats and flinging articles of clothing as they progressed down the pier in the expectation that someone else would pick up after them"?

Bobby never would've heard the end of it.

He lay there and thought about Special Ed. And for the first time in days, Bobby smiled. He pictured Special Ed striding up and down the freight dock with his belly poking through his T-shirt. ("Drinking beer helps keep my weight up," he liked to say.) And the way he drove through the city, honking and swearing at all the cars, even flipping off the one-way street signs. And telling stories about the crazy things he'd done. Like when he worked in San Diego for a piano-moving firm and one day at these fancy apartments, he purposely dropped an upright off a hoist so he could watch it tumble into the swimming pool.

Bobby tried to imagine having pulled off that prank, but he never could've been so free and easy. No Kennedy could, except maybe Jack. But Bobby was a prude compared to Jack. Which perhaps explains why he felt such an affinity for rascals like Special Ed. They did things he couldn't. They weren't burdened like he was. They helped him to forget his special destiny.

Paul Corbin was another example. Now there was a rogue who had style. Or so Bobby thought. Kenny O'Donnell despised him. All the guys around Jack had despised him. They had viewed him, correctly, as a political liability.

Still, Bobby had a soft spot for Paul Corbin. He loved to hear the gossip about his exploits. Take what he did back in 1960. This was during the Wisconsin primary. Jack and Hubert Humphrey were going head to head, and what with Wisconsin being Hubert's backyard, things weren't looking too good for Jack. Everyone was saying no Catholic could win, so Corbin tried to remedy the matter. He did this by sending a vicious anti-Catholic pamphlet to every Catholic household in Wisconsin. And he mailed the pamphlet from Hubert's home state to make it look like Humphrey forces were responsible.

Well you should've heard Hubert whine! But the more he complained, the more the Catholics believed he really was behind the hate-filled mailing. And sure enough, in spite of conventional wisdom, many Catholic Republicans crossed over: they voted for Jack in the Democratic primary, and Jack whipped Hubert's sorry ass.

And then there was the embassy scam. It seems that Paul Corbin raised money for Jack by promising jobs to potential donors. And the job he was fondest of giving away was the ambassadorship to Ecuador. But after Corbin gave that post to three men in one town—the police chief, the mayor, and the funeral director— Bobby was forced to call Corbin up and instruct him to diversify his offerings.

Those were the days, Bobby thought. And after Jack won they got better. At least for a while they got better. For back then he wasn't plagued by self-doubt, remorse, compassion, and other byproducts of maturity.

Bobby thought about that time before the anguish set in. He remembered a typical morning: chewing out the head of the CIA over breakfast for making the country (and by implication the President) look bad by screwing up the Bay of Pigs invasion; chewing out the Joint Chiefs of Staff after breakfast for potentially making the country (and by implication the President) look bad by supplying only three days' worth of ammunition to our conventional forces in Berlin; calling up the governor of Louisiana to chew him out for making the country (and by implication the President) look bad by defying a judge's order to desegregate the schools; chewing out some Negro leaders over coffee for making the country (and by implication the President) look bad by deemphasizing the quiet if pragmatic route of voter registration in favor of such high-profile tactics as escorting little Negro children past mobs of frenzied whites in order to enroll them in public schools; chewing out a delegation of southern congressmen for making the country (and by implication the President) look bad by not exhorting their white constituents to stop gathering in mobs to curse at and spit upon innocent Negro school children; calling up an influential TV news executive to chew him out for making the country (and by implication the President) look bad by airing footage of white mobs down south; and chewing out several prominent liberals over lunch for making the President (and by implication the country) look bad by asserting that the White House course on civil rights was determined by political rather than moral imperatives.

Lunch was followed by a quick phone call to Marilyn Monroe to plan their next tryst; a longer phone call to Adlai Stevenson in New York to chew him out for no particular reason except being generally soft on everything; a covert meeting in an underground garage with KGB agent Georgi Bolshakov to exchange secret messages between President Kennedy and Chairman Khrushchev; and a return to the Justice Department to hold a strategy session with the eighteen crack lawyers and investigators who composed the Get Hoffa Squad.

Those really were the days, Bobby thought. He mused about Jimmy Hoffa. Which made him think about Santos Trafficante. Which made him think about Johnny Roselli. Which made him think about Carlos Marcello. Which made him think about David Ferrie. Which made him think about the smoke and the popping sounds that had come from the grassy knoll. And the way that Jack's skull had erupted in a burst of bone, blood, and blue-gray brains.

Bobby got a pain in his head.

Meanwhile, Gerbil was alone at his station, watching Bobby on the closed-circuit monitor. Gerbil found the sight of the prone, helpless man to be intriguing, even arousing. In fact, he greatly desired to march into the cell and fuck the shit out of Bobby Kennedy. But leaving his station was a risky proposition since it could lead to a reprimand from his superiors. So to be on the safe side, instead of raping Bobby Kennedy, Gerbil jerked off into a napkin. Then he zipped up his fly and ate a corn dog for dinner.

As for Bobby, he was trying to refocus. He was trying to conjure up a pleasant memory or two, and he thought about his kids when they were young. He remembered coming home to Hickory Hill and hugging his kids by the armload. He remembered the way they slept: clutching their teddies and sucking their thumbs, speaking strange words now and then. He remembered picking Courtney up on a soft July night during Jack's first summer as President. He hefted the tiny girl over his head and told her to reach for the sky. "I touched the stars, Daddy. I *felt* them," she said.

God, he had loved his kids.

Bobby lay there and stared at the wall. And the concrete wall slowly melted away and turned into a child's bedroom. Bobby saw himself holding David when David was four. David the shy one, the runt. David the child Bobby understood best. "Daddy, don't go," he was saying.

"I have to catch a plane," Bobby said.

David shook his head. "You don't have to," he said. "You don't have to go if you don't want to."

"I have to help Uncle Jack become President." It was December of 1959.

"If you stay here I'll draw you a picture," David said. Bobby kissed his little boy and set him down.

"I'll put two angels in the picture," David said.

Bobby watched himself leave the room. And he saw his son standing there, crying. Then David faded away and was replaced by a hearse. It was 1984. It was David's funeral.

Bobby closed his eyes and groaned. Now he had a truly vicious headache. He squeezed his temples with his hands and groaned some more. But the pain didn't go away. It just changed from a throb to a sizzle. It was like Bobby's head had turned into a toaster, and red-hot wires were implanted in his skull. He grabbed at his hair and saw flashes and pops, tiny flares and fleeting visions from long ago.

The first fleeting vision was of Jack. Of Jack in a White House bed. Of Jack and two blondes in a huge White House bed, a tangle of arms and legs and tits and asses. One of the blondes had gone down on Jack while

Jack kissed the other and stroked her breasts.

Who were those blondes, Bobby wondered. Then the one giving head looked up for a minute and Bobby remembered the face. It was the girl known as Fiddle. Or was it Faddle? It was *one* of those blondes from the secretarial pool who Kenny O'Donnell and the others made crude jokes about. Bobby felt embarrassed for Jack. He looked so undignified, so unpresidential. He looked like a goddamned fool.

Then Fiddle—or was it Faddle?—went back to work. She bobbed up and down and Jack closed his eyes. Jesus fucking Christ, Bobby thought. The fire in his skull was burning out. But he was still seeing flashes and pops. Time moved forward several years to '64. He recognized the Oval Office. He saw a tall ugly man and a short ugly man leaning over the President's desk. There was a small tape recorder on the desk. The two men were listening as it played. And they were grinning and cackling and nudging each other like schoolboys with a dirty magazine.

Bobby peered more closely at the men. One of them was Lyndon Baines Johnson. The other was J. Edgar Hoover. My God they are ugly, Bobby thought.

He heard sounds from the tape, some gasps and some moans. "Yes! Yes!" a woman was saying. "Oh!

Oh!" said a man. "Deeper! Deeper!" said the woman.

Bobby figured it was Jack with Judith Campbell. Or maybe it was Jack with Angie Dickinson. Or with Fiddle or Faddle. Or Marilyn Monroe. Or Mary Meyer. Or Inga-Binga. Or someone else. Then again, perhaps it was Martin Luther King holding one of his post-rally orgies. Or was it Bobby himself that one time he stepped out?

"This'll fix the little fart," Lyndon said.

Jesus Christ, had they gotten Hoffa's tape? The one he made of Bobby and Marilyn that included the lovemaking sounds? Bobby went back to when Jack was still President, and he saw himself kissing Marilyn. They were naked, in bed, at Peter Lawford's house. Marilyn turned onto her stomach. She looked over her shoulder and smiled at Bobby. They went at it like doggies.

Bobby blushed.

He opened his eyes to make the vision go away, but he didn't see the concrete wall. Instead he saw a movie that leapfrogged backward in time, starting with David again. "Please don't go, Daddy," David said. "I'll draw you a picture. I'll put two angels in the picture."

Bobby saw his son standing there, crying. Then he saw himself when he was young. He was a little boy of

70

four back in Bronxville. He was sitting on the steps, the broad front steps, waiting for Jack to get home. Waiting and hoping that Jack would take him for a walk and tell him tales about knights and dragons.

What a sad little boy, Bobby thought. But then he saw something sadder still. It was Daddy, when Daddy was young. He was standing alone in *his* daddy's saloon, dressed in short pants and a cap. He was greedily eating a piece of chocolate.

There's nothing sad about that, Bobby thought. All little boys eat chocolate. So why did it make him so sad? Bobby had no idea. But watching the boy lick the chocolate off his fingers made Bobby swallow hard and almost cry.

As for Gerbil, he was scratching his balls. And regretting the fact that he'd exercised prudence by jerking off a short while ago. After all, Bobby Kennedy had spat in his face. The scumbag *deserved* to be raped.

But now Gerbil couldn't get it up. And by the time the old hormones had had a chance to recoup, to give him a no-nonsense hard-on, his shift would be over for the day.

Gerbil sat back and loudly broke wind. He wasn't very pleased with his pecker. He hated his life. He hated the world. And above all he hated Bobby Kennedy.

In this respect the fat guard was hardly singular. In fact just at that moment, as Bobby stared at the wall, the picture he was viewing jumped forward. It was 1957 in the halls of the Senate. Or at least it looked like the halls of the Senate. The marble; the portraits; the dark, heavy wood. Yes, it was definitely the United States Senate. Except that dogs aren't allowed in the Senate. And there were two dogs, boy dogs. They were fierce-looking bulldogs who circled each other. They sniffed each other's crotches. They growled.

"My name is Jimmy Hoffa," said one of the dogs.

"You don't look tough to me," said the other.

The boy dog named Jimmy raised his hind leg and said, "Well, you look like a hydrant to me!" Then he pissed in the other dog's face.

But we were *people*, Bobby thought as he remembered that encounter, the first time he'd set eyes on Jimmy Hoffa. We were people, not dogs, Bobby thought. And while it's true he'd told Jimmy, "You don't look tough to me," Jimmy hadn't made water in his face. He'd just glowered in a provocative manner. Whereupon, right there, in the halls of the Senate, Bobby had challenged him to a push-up contest.

So okay, Bobby thought, I was immature. But we

were *people,* he thought, as he stared at the dogs.

The picture jumped forward. He saw people. It was 1962 in his office at Justice. He saw himself and several aides. It was late. He had rolled up his shirtsleeves. This was an action-packed night: all hell was breaking loose in Alabama.

Bobby heard himself talking on the phone. To Martin Luther King, who was inside a church, surrounded by a mob of frenzied whites. To John Patterson, the governor, who was throwing a fit about the presence of federal marshals. To this one and that one. To key men in the field. "Yes, now!" Bobby snapped. "Just do it!"

He was all of thirty-six years old. And he was managing the biggest crisis in America. And managing it deftly at that.

Bobby stroked the green beret on his desk. It was sturdily made yet soft to the touch.

The phone rang again. It was the governor.

Poor John Patterson, Bobby thought. He'd endorsed Jack way back in '59. He'd endorsed the young Catholic from up north. It was a very risky move for a southern governor to make. And very helpful, from the Kennedys' point of view. It had broken the South wide open.

But now the election was over. So they no longer

needed John's unswerving loyalty. So they could screw him if they had to.

So they did.

They brought in the marshals to save Martin's life. And in so doing they raised the specter of Reconstruction.

Boy, was John Patterson mad. "No white man will ever vote for me again. And no Negro ever did in the first place!"

Bobby shrugged. John was right. He was lunch meat.

"We won't let you do this. The South will fight back!"

"Save the speeches for the locals," Bobby said. He fingered the felt beret.

Expendable John bent his ear for another hour. Then Martin Luther King got on the horn. He was still in the church, still trapped by the mob, with only Bobby's marshals to protect him. Yet instead of thanking Bobby, he got angry. "What ever happened to law and order?" Martin said. "Can't a man leave a church in this country?"

"You'd be as dead as Kelsey's nuts without them."

"Excuse me?" said Martin.

"Without the marshals," Bobby said. "You'd be

deader than his nuts."

"Who's Kelsey?"

"That's a good question, Martin. I don't know. Still, it's safe to assume that he's dead."

Bobby had respect for Dr. King. But sometimes he found him to be exasperating. Why couldn't he wait until Jack's second term? He was giving propaganda to the Russians. "All these riots," said Bobby. "They're embarrassing Jack.'"

"We've been embarrassed all our lives," Martin said.

Bobby thought about that. It was not a bad point. In fact, it was an excellent point. His hard eyes grew soft for a moment. "We're doing everything we can," he said. Then he eased the phone back into its cradle. He stretched out his arms. He looked around at his aides. It was a quarter to five in the morning.

We are young, Bobby thought. We are young, tough, and ready. He gazed at the felt green beret. How vital it looked! So manly, so sleek.

They were Bobby's pet project, these berets. Not the actual hats, but the soldiers who wore them. Yes, Bobby was the man on Special Forces: the administration's chief proponent of counter-insurgency; of cultivating home-grown guerrillas. We would show all the scoffers that our boys had guts, too; that they could live in the jungles like the Russians. And our boys would eat snakes with *more* gusto and zest than Nikita's jungle warriors ever did. We would win hearts and minds. We would win the whole world!

At least that was the basic game plan for hegemony. And the Special Forces were the linchpins of the plan. "They are my babies," Bobby thought, "my special babies."

Speaking of which, he saw a dead one on his desk. Right where the beret used to be. It was a dead, bloody baby of Asian descent.

Bobby gasped. His aides turned. Bobby pointed. And they saw what he saw, which was a felt green beret.

"Hey Bob, you okay?" Burke Marshall asked.

"I'm fine," Bobby said, although he looked kind of pale. "Just dreaming, that's all," Bobby muttered.

But of course he wasn't dreaming; he was hallucinating. He was lying in a cell in 1989. He hadn't eaten for days. He was dehydrated. A fat guard named Gerbil, who'd been deprived of a rape, and consequently was determined to avenge himself, watched Bobby on closed-circuit TV. And as he watched he began to conceive of a plan that would make Bobby Kennedy crazy. He would fuck Bobby's mind; push him over the edge. A psychological rape, so to speak.

To be sure, this was not Gerbil's torture of choice. He was kind of old-fashioned in that regard. He preferred the traditional physical rapes. But if he had to go psychological, so be it.

As for his target—the reincarnated Bobby—he was pretty easy pickings for a mindfuck. I mean the guy was half-loony already. Or maybe even three-quarters gone. For example, as he looked at a concrete wall that was speckled here and there with shit and blood, what he saw was the Justice Department. Yes, he was still in his office in 1962, still fixated on the beret.

Happily for Bobby, the beret on his desk was no longer a dead Asian baby. Unhappily for Bobby, it was reproducing. First the beret split in two. Then the two split again to make four. And those four split in two, and those eight split in two, and so it progressed geometrically.

In no time at all half a million berets were marching across Bobby's desk. And the berets became men fighting battles. Bobby saw Tet. He saw Hamburger Hill. He saw U.S. Marines without heads. And grunts without arms. He saw guts spilling out—intestines, for the most part, but also livers. And an occasional kidney or section of lung. Men were crying for their mothers. They were howling. They yammered and bleated for all they were worth.

A ruptured spleen floated by in the muck. It was followed by a still-beating heart. Then a stray set of eyes, three wiggling toes, a big chunk of thigh, and two necks.

Bobby's desk had turned into a rendering plant. A human rendering plant. Bobby blanched. He looked wildly around but his aides had gone home. So there was no one to say, "You okay?" There was no one to stop him from seeing what he saw.

He turned back to the rendering plant. And all he saw was his desk, his unadorned desk, with the exception, of course, of that beret. It was just a felt green beret like any other. But Bobby didn't trust the little fucker. He wanted to burn it or shred it to bits. Or at least get it out of his sight.

Bobby tried to reach for the beret. He planned to fling it, like a Frisbee, out the window. But his arms wouldn't budge from his sides. It was as if they'd become someone else's. It was as if he was four and playing football with Joe while Daddy looked on from the porch. Bobby's arms were just big, useless clunks.

He sat back defeated, resigned. And he started to think about Daddy. About Daddy the lecher and Daddy the crook and Daddy the Nazi apologist.

It would be nice to blame his problems on Daddy. But the berets weren't his daddy's idea. What did Pop know about counter-insurgency? The man didn't know boo, Bobby thought. He was stroked out in a wheelchair in Hyannis. He was rolling his eyes and speaking in tongues.

Bobby wept for his paralyzed daddy.

Gerbil noticed that Bobby had shifted positions, and that he appeared to be moaning and crying. Gerbil was glad that Bobby was conscious since he'd be no fun to torture if he passed out. Well maybe a little fun, but not a whole lot of fun.

Gerbil wondered what Bobby was thinking. Now that's a luxury item—the act of wonder. For someone like Bobby there was no wonder left. There was no energy for anything left. So he was viewing, that's all, simply taking it in. And there was certainly no shortage of prime-time specials. You see, that vision on the wall had become those visions on the walls, and on the floor and on the ceiling as well. Different movies, wherever he looked!

Over here, for example, was a chemist. He had a cultivated air, this chemist: quiet, bespectacled, a man who read books. Just the opposite of crude, vulgar

Gerbil. He kind of looked like Mac Bundy's shy colleague from Harvard. What was his name? Henry
Kissinger?

He was working in a lab, this cultivated chemist, and
he was clearly absorbed by a problem. His eyes seemed
to shine with intellectual vigor as he went about his
scientific business: stirring solutions, filling up beakers,
figuring out complex equations.

In a way, Bobby envied the man: to derive satisfaction
from basic research, to find beauty in the periodic table.
To not be consumed with saving the world. To go home
to his wife. To mow the lawn.

A simple life, Bobby thought. An unsullied life. He
watched the chemist cross the lab to a cage. He watched
him open the cage and pull out a baby. It was a live Asian
baby. It was squalling.

"Oh no," Bobby groaned, but the chemist paid no
heed. Mad scientists in movies never do.

Bobby turned to the film on the opposite wall. He was
hoping it would be a different genre. And for once
Bobby seemed to be in luck: it appeared to be your
basic Central American jungle thriller, replete with
snakes and hanging clusters of bananas. Exotic birds
squawked, machetes slashed through the brush, and
Bobby let out a sigh of relief. He imagined himself

eating popcorn. He thought about sailing and skiing and scotch, about just kicking back and having fun.

But then he tensed up again. For when the camera zoomed in on the star of the movie, it turned out to be Carlos Marcello! Yes, the Mafia chieftain was playing himself, and he was not in a very good mood. In fact, his state of mind was downright foul. He was trudging through the jungle in a suit and a tie, sweating profusely and cussing. He cussed everything and everyone under the sun, but his extra-special cusses were for Bobby.

Marcello's reasons for cussing were sound. It was April of 1961. And Bobby, who had just become the nation's top prosecutor, had revived an old deportation order. He had had Carlos flown to Guatemala of all places, and the Guatemalans had expelled him to El Salvador. The Salvadorans, in turn, had dropped him off in the jungle. And now he was walking home.

At the time it had seemed like a capital idea—to let Carlos know who was boss. To send him off without so much as a clean pair of socks.

But that was just the start of the movie. Bobby thought about the scenes that would come next: Marilyn's death, the killing of Jack, his own murder at the hands of Eugene Thane Cesar. Not to mention his numerous regrettable acts during the course of his present incarnation.

And all because he'd messed with Carlos Marcello in a way that was intended to provoke. Why couldn't he just have indicted the guy like a normal attorney general would? And then winked when his lawyers got him off on a technicality. And then met him for a golf game in Vegas.

Whatever possessed him to fuck with Marcello?

Moral outrage, Bobby thought. Moral outrage.

That's what Marilyn said she loved about him most— that he still had the capacity for outrage.

She'd been sucking him off at the time. Then she'd stopped to catch her breath and muse out loud. She put her head on his belly and talked. His older brother, the President, was smoother, she said. Better looking. More witty by far. But moral outrage was no longer a part of Jack's repertoire. If it had ever been there in the first place, Marilyn said.

Bobby shrugged and felt flattered. He was in love. He looked at that face, that incredible face. He took her head in his hands. He stroked her hair. She smelled of honey and woman and everything good. Plus something else he couldn't name, something wild. Something that allowed him to forget who he was, but at another, deeper level, to remember. And which made it okay to have failed miserably as a paperboy, and to have dropped all those passes in front of Daddy. And to wonder if maybe Jack *did* have some problems. Psychological, not political, that is.

Bobby caught himself having these thoughts. "I must be getting soft," he said to himself. "If I don't watch it, I'll feel sympathy for Adlai!"

Little did he know about how soft and kind and wise he would become in the ensuing six years. Little did he know what lay in store!

Marilyn inched up and placed her head on his chest. She gave him a curious look. "I have a question about men," she said.

Bobby cuddled her breasts, perfect fistfuls of magic. "Ask me anything you want," he said.

"Why are they obsessed with fellatio?"

"Excuse me?" he said.

"With blowjobs," she said. "That's all they live for: getting head. To have a blonde with big tits put her lips on their cock. What's so great about that?" she said.

Bobby thought about that, and then he said something clever; almost as clever as something Jack might've said. "It tends to end a lot of arguments," Bobby said.

Bobby lay there and thought about Marilyn. They'd

done some crazy things together. Truly crazy. Like that time she'd dared him to risk his career by donning a fake beard and sunglasses, and then going for a walk on a beach for nude bathers. "I *double* dare you," she said. "And I'll go with you!"

He remembered the day. He remembered the sun. He remembered the sand between his toes. And how his plumbing had dangled as he strolled, *incognito*, with Marilyn, in a kerchief, on his arm.

They sure pulled one over on that beach full of nudists. Not to mention the entire American public! Then she died. And he died. And came back to life.

Bobby returned to the present. But the present was the past, of course. For as he lay in his cell he was watching a movie set in April of 1961. He saw Carlos Marcello emerge from the jungle, walk into a phone booth, and throw a tantrum. Carlos jumped up and down as he screamed at the mouthpiece. He heaped oath after oath upon Bobby. And insisted that someone should whack Bobby's boss.

Bobby turned onto his back. Perhaps the movie on the ceiling would be better. Unfortunately, however, it wasn't. It was the goddamned mad scientist again. Bobby looked to the wall on his left. Then he looked to the wall on his right. He craned his neck for a glimpse of the wall behind his head. He checked the wall beyond his feet. He checked the floor. He even closed his eyes to scan the movie in his mind. That's seven separate theaters, in case you're counting. And the mad-scientist feature was playing in every one!

What ever happened to variety, Bobby wondered. What ever happened to freedom of choice? What ever happened to the basic civil rights and guarantees that were set forth in the United States Constitution? Hadn't his keepers ever read the fucking thing?

Bobby saw himself posing that question to a sheriff who'd been harassing Cesar Chavez and his people. This was back in California in '66. And this sheriff had been rounding up striking grape pickers and hauling them off to jail. He'd been doing it for reasons of safety, he said. He'd been making *preventive* arrests.

That's when Bobby had asked him if he'd ever read the Constitution. But Bobby was a senator then. And senators can ask acid questions of sheriffs without fear of getting clobbered by a nightstick.

Good old power, Bobby thought. Good old power. To be sure, it has pitfalls and drawbacks. But at least when you have it you don't go around scared.

Unless you're plagued by inner demons, that is. Like Nixon. Or Johnson. Or Bobby himself on those occasions when he'd lost touch with his good instincts. For example, in the fall of '67. His instincts said do it, just take Lyndon on, but his advisers said no, you can't run. The old advisers, at any rate, such as Sorenson. And Kenny O'Donnell and the rest of Jack's boys. So Bobby had waffled for months. And in the process he'd permitted Eugene McCarthy to enter first.

Bobby thought about that Minnesota pissant. And about how lonely he'd felt over Christmas that year as all the liberals had flocked to lazy Gene. And how much he'd missed Jack as events passed him by. And how much he'd missed Daddy's strong hand.

Then one night he dreamed about Marilyn. "Just do it!" she said.

So he did.

He remembered the day he announced. And his sense of release once the battle was joined. And how they'd mobbed him in the ghettos in '68. They tore at his clothes; they ripped into his soul.

Of course he no longer fed off crowds. Being dead had put a *few* things in perspective. Yes, getting shot in the head at the Ambassador Hotel can cure a man of his ambition in a hurry! A corpse doesn't care about delegate counts, and is pretty much immune to adulation. And resurrection hadn't served to awaken the lure: Bobby still had no desire to press the flesh. Indeed, at this point in his second career, a crush of voters would only make him agoraphobic But he wished he had someone, *one person*, to touch. Or if not a human being, at least a puppy. And a fraction, the merest fraction, of a senator's pull. Just enough to choose which movie he would see.

Bobby sighed and stared up at the ceiling. The mad scientist was stirring two beakers. The camera zoomed in on the beakers. One of them was labeled POLYSTY-RENE. The other one was labeled WHITE PHOSPHO-RUS.

The beakers and their labels faded out. They were replaced by a U.S. bomber pilot. He was talking to a British photojournalist. It was 1966 in Da Nang, Vietnam, and the topic of discussion was napalm. "Now don't get me wrong," the pilot was saying. "We're fond of those boys back at Dow. But the original product had defects. If the target was quick—and Victor Charlie is quick—he could flick the stuff off like hard snot. So the boys back at Dow started adding polystyrene, and now it sticks just like shit to a blanket. Then they added Willie Peter—white phosphorus, that is—so the gooks couldn't jump in the river. I mean they could but it burns under water. And one drop's enough; it burns down to the bone. Willie Peter is no good for Victor's health."

"You mean it kills him?"

"By poison. It might take a few weeks, but what's the rush so long as Charles gets the grease?"

"Thank you for your time," said the British photo-journalist.

The pilot mugged for the camera. He said, "Hi, Ma."

On the floor of his cell Bobby Kennedy prayed. He asked God if he would please change the movie. He said three Hail Marys. He said, "I promise to be good." He said, "I'm sorry for poking Chester in the belly. And for shooting Marcello. And for botching the job. And for other sins too numerous to mention."

"Like what?" said a voice.

"Is the correct answer *hubris?*"

"Too pat," said the voice inside his head.

"Adultery?"

"No. Well, maybe a little. I guess I'll have to think about that."

"Civil rights? Vietnam?"

"Hard to say," said the voice.

"Can you give me a hint?"

"I'd rather not."

"Shit," Bobby said.

"Be cool," said the voice.

The mad-scientist movie stopped playing. It simply froze in mid-frame. Then it vanished.

And was followed by an ever-so-brief intermission.

Which was followed by another goddamned movie.

This new goddamned movie was the home film variety, the prevideo home film variety: silent and jerky and chronologically skewed. It seemed to hopscotch through time like a spastic.

Beginning with a glimpse of Bobby's grandpa, Honey Fitz, back when Grandpa was the mayor of Boston. It was summer and he looked natty in a white ice cream suit. He was standing on the steps of City Hall. He moved his arms up and down as he spoke to a crowd. He ended his speech with a flourish. He waved his straw hat. The people waved back. It was the start of the American Century.

The picture jumped ahead to 1960. Bobby's little boy, David, was nesting in bed, surrounded by all his stuffed animals. He clutched a giraffe and appeared to be singing. Sure enough, a little bubble appeared. It bounced merrily above the words of a song the little boy was singing to himself. It was a song about the people and beings he loved, and who loved him in return. It went, "Daddy and Mommy and Brumus the Dog and Mickey Mouse and Jesus and My Dinger."

On the floor of his cell, Bobby smiled. And stopped smiling when the picture jumped forward. It was 1984 in an autopsy room. The pathologist was slicing David's stomach.

Then it was 1968 in an autopsy room, and the pathologist was slicing Bobby's skull.

Then it was 1963 in an autopsy room, and a navy surgeon was dissecting Jack's brain. Or what was left of Jack's brain, at any rate. "Not much to work with," the surgeon remarked as he reached for the jar of formaldehyde.

"Oh God," Bobby said.

It was 1962, and they were slicing Marilyn open with a buzz saw.

"No, no," Bobby said.

The picture jumped back. He saw Daddy climb in bed with Gloria Swanson.

The picture jumped forward. It was late at night in Hyannis. Daddy opened a bedroom door. Bobby watched as his daddy crept into the room and woke up the guest, a young woman. She was a very young woman, no more than eighteen. She was a friend of Kathleen's from the convent. Bobby watched as the ambassador to the Court of St. James put the moves on this petrified child. Bobby watched as she fought Daddy off.

The old family movie jumped back. There was Grandpa again, on a dance floor in Boston. He was dancing with Toodles O'Ryan. He was kissing the large-chested cigarette girl. He was trying to cop a feel.

The picture jumped forward and Bobby saw his own kids, behaving like the rich brats they were: cutting in ski lines at Waterville Valley.

It was 1968 in Watts. A woman grabbed his cuff links. A kid took his shoes.

It was primary night in California. A security guard named Eugene Thane Cesar shot Bobby point-blank in the head. Bobby grabbed Cesar's tie. Bobby fell to the floor. Bobby lay on his back.

Bobby dreamed.

He traveled all the way back to his boyhood in Bronxville while the surgeons groped inside his ruined brain. It was eight thirty-five, just after his bedtime. The nurse had tucked him in at eight-thirty. Then she'd shut off his light, walked down the wide stairs, and returned to her quarters for the night.

Bobby lay still. He heard sounds in his mind, the usual buzzes and hums. But no grown-up sounds; no foot-steps or voices. No bath water running. The coast was clear.

Bobby reached for the large Army flashlight beneath

his bed. He gripped the metal handle with both hands. Then he climbed out of bed and walked on tiptoes across the room. He shined the flashlight at his good friend, the goldfish. This goldfish and Bobby were very good friends. In fact, she was his best friend in the world.

He had named her "Oriet" almost six years ago, back when he had gotten her for Christmas. She'd arrived as a baby, but now she was old. She waved her long, thin, silver fins. She swam up and nuzzled the edge of the bowl. She kissed Bobby "Hello" through the glass.

"Hello," Bobby said with his thoughts.

That's how they talked, just with thoughts. They often held solemn conversations. Especially when Bobby felt troubled. Like when he couldn't catch a football in front of Daddy or Joe. Or when he noticed that his face looked like a rabbit's. Or when he realized that he'd always be stuck with himself, instead of turning into Jack and vice versa.

Not to mention his most recent and biggest disgrace, the most shameful event of his life: he'd been forced to repeat the third grade. He was telling Oriet all about it. About how stupid he was, how he hated himself, how he wished that he'd never been born.

Oriet listened and then she said that she loved him. She told him, "I'll always be here."

"In the bowl?" Bobby said.

"And outside the bowl. I'll always be watching for you."

"Like an angel?" he said.

"Exactly," she said.

She started swimming in circles, which was the signal. It was time to start playing the game. The way the game went was like this: Bobby would make a cup with his hand, and stick it in Oriet's bowl. Oriet would swim into the cup. Then Bobby would rotate his hand cup around, sculling water and the goldfish simultaneously.

Near the end of the game he would uncup his hand while easing it up to the edge. And at the very last second, as his palm touched the glass, Oriet would effect an escape: she would dart through a space between Bobby's splayed fingers.

Only this time, she missed. Or he did. Instead of feeling glass at the end of the game, Bobby's palm came in contact with the fish. And it was not just her tail or a sliver of fin. He had squashed Oriet through the middle! Bobby withdrew his hand from the bowl. He let it hang in midair, dripping water.

On the floor of his cell Bobby Kennedy squirmed as he relived that horrible night. He stared up at the movie that was playing on the ceiling, the movie that was starring himself. The child star, little Bobby, stood trans-fixed. In his left hand he clutched an amphibious flash-light. His right hand—the deadly weapon—hung inert. And his eyes were locked in to the eyes of his fish as she arched back and forth in her agony. With each painful spasm she sank slowly down. As death-throe scenes go, it was a doozy.

At last Oriet reached the bottom of the bowl where she continued to jerk and blow bubbles. In addition she was spurting a stream of fish blood mixed with small but vital bits of goldfish innards.

A thin beam of light shot out from her eyes and made contact with young Bobby's eyes. In movie parlance this beam was supposed to suggest a magical transfer of thought. Which is what, in real life, was taking place. Oriet was begging Bobby for mercy. "Please kill me," she said. "It hurts."

"But how?" Bobby said.

"With the flashlight," she said.

"I can't," Bobby said.

"Yes you can."

The little boy in the movie was terrified. But he willed himself into action. He wrapped his right hand around the thick flashlight handle. He lifted the blunt, heavy object. He positioned his cudgel right over the bowl.

"Hurry up!" said the fish.

Bobby plunged. He felt the flashlight strike home. He felt Oriet flail. Bobby cringed and pressed harder. He twisted down. He ground his best friend into Oriet pulp.

"Thank you," she said as she expired.

There was another intermission on the ceiling. The little boy and the fish were replaced by a cup of sparkling, cool, refreshing, tasty Coke. It seemed to froth with patriotic strength and fervor. Then the Coke faded out and was replaced by a line of brightly colored Peanut M&M's. They performed a short jig which led them off to stage right where a tub of buttered popcorn bowed and smiled.

Advertisingwise, the point was clear. And perhaps a different viewer would've taken the hint and gotten up to buy himself a treat. Or at least commenced to salivate. Or thought, "Yum yum." But what with the dearth of concession stands in the intensive management unit—and the fact that he was half-dead and distraught—inmate Kennedy wasn't lured by thoughts of food. He simply picked up where the movie left off, projecting scenes upon the big screen in his mind.

Beginning with the one in which he ran down the hall

and darted into the children's bathroom. He saw himself turn on the faucet full force. He saw himself scrubbing the flashlight. Then he watched as he scampered downstairs in search of Mother.

Bobby found her in the parlor. She was reading. Or pretending to read, at any rate. Actually, she'd been stuck on one page for an hour. She'd been thinking about Gloria Swanson. She'd been thinking about all of her husband's affairs. She'd been mired in anger and grief.

But what did Bobby care or even know about philandering? All he knew was that he had to confess. And since Jack was at school and the priest was at church, he poured out his story to Mother. He told the whole thing, A to Z. He talked about how awful and worthless he was. He said that he—not the fish—deserved to die.

Water dripped from his flashlight as he spoke. Mother noticed the spots that appeared on the rug, a priceless work of art from ancient Persia. She thought about licentiousness. She thought about men. She thought about how boys turn into men.

"Well," she inquired when Bobby's tale was done, "what lesson did you learn from all of this?"

"That I am evil," he said as he stared at his feet.

"And to follow the rules," added Mother. "If you

sneak out of bed, bad things happen."

Intermission on the ceiling was over. The old family movie resumed. Bobby watched as the little boy climbed the wide stairs. Bobby watched as he entered his room. Bobby watched as he turned on his large Army flashlight and slowly advanced on the fishbowl.

The camera panned the water in the bowl. There were entrails here and entrails there. There were pieces of fin on the surface. They floated like lilies.

The camera moved down. The bottom of the bowl was a mess: a grab bag of scales, miscellaneous guts, busted gills, and other signs of goldfish carnage. For example, an unattached eye. It was sitting by a pile of broken cartilage.

The camera zoomed in on the eye. Inside the eye, there were visions.

The first vision showed a young man poke an old man in the belly. "As of now you were all for it," said the upstart.

The next vision was of vanity in action. A witty and handsome and horny chief executive was standing by a bucket of hand-stitched baseballs. It was April in the White House back yard. The following day the man would throw out the first ball of the major-league season.

Many voters would see him do it on the news. And he desired their allegiance, of course. But what he craved, above all, was a silky-smooth motion; to look as graceful as Sandy Koufax on TV. So the sexy Young Prez bent down for a ball.

And turned into a blonde on a floor. She was gorgeous and dead.

She turned into a train. There was a coffin in the very last car.

There were crowds by the tracks. They lined either side. They became a bunch of people at a party. It was a victory party at the Ambassador Hotel.

There were shots.

There were screams.

There were sirens.

And the obligatory blood. And the obligatory brains, oozing out like crusty toothpaste from a tube.

The camera pulled back from the fishbowl. The child star, little Bobby, reappeared. He was staring at the visions in Oriet's eye. He was utterly bewildered by what he saw.

Which was not, sad to say, a state of mind being offered by the Great Mental Menu in the cell. Not even in the A la Carte or Side Order sections. No Psychic

Shield Due to Ignorance and Youth.

The only item, in fact, for Bobby's mind to ingest was a new and crushing insight about his defects: there was no way to balance things out. There was no way to cancel his sins. Because he couldn't begin. Because nobody can.

Good works are good works, Bobby thought. And bad works are bad works.

And they're separate.

So even if he'd managed to make Hoffa squirm or raise a few hopes in the ghettos, or save a few backs in the moving-man trade or stand up for Noodle in the joint, Bobby couldn't unsquash Oriet. Or unpoke Chester Bowles. Or uncheat on his wife.

Not to mention being rude to Tip O'Neill.

He couldn't force Jack to unfuck his chippies and he couldn't take the bully out of Daddy. He couldn't assume the family shame, or undo the damage done by trying.

Speaking of which, what hurt most of all was that he couldn't unsuicide Marilyn.

The projectionist switched movies again. And wouldn't you know, with the luck he'd been having, Bobby's least favorite feature returned. Yes, The Green Beret from Hell was on the ceiling. Bobby recognized his office back at Justice. As always, the beret was on his desk. To the right of the beret was his own private phone, the one used for Jack and other intimates. And sitting in a chair was the attorney general himself, staring at the special private line.

It was high summer of 1962. Bobby's aides were all gone and Ethel was waiting. She'd been waiting for several hours, in fact. He had promised to be home by six o'clock. But Bobby was hoping that his special line would ring. He was yearning for Marilyn's voice.

Of course he knew she wouldn't call because she couldn't. He had changed his private number to make sure she couldn't call. But love being what it is, he chose to hope.

The man in the chair picked up the receiver. He started to dial her number. Then he put the phone down. And picked it up. And put it down.

"Pathetic," Bobby thought. "Just pathetic."

Suddenly, the movie got busy. Thousands of newspapers rolled off a press. Huge banner headlines filled the cell: MARILYN DEAD. AMERICA MOURNS. RARE PHOTOS INSIDE.

And so forth. Announcers announced and newsboys cried "EXTRA!"

There was a grave.

There were some mourners.

And there was Bobby. He was sitting in his office in mid-September. He was staring at his special, private line. The woman was dead. She'd been dead for a month. The phone didn't ring.

Bobby stared.

As he lay in his cell and remembered that time, he remembered another time. It was back when he was mourning Oriet. Every night after prayers he shivered in bed, fearing her eye would come to haunt him. And hoping that her voice would come to soothe him.

Bobby wondered if the movie would return to Oriet, to those visions in her unattached eye. But for once the bastards stuck with the program: it was The Green Beret from Hell all the way.

The man at the desk stared down at his phone. Then the camera zoomed in on the beret. Slowly, the beret began to jiggle. And to get longer and thinner at one end. The long and thin end acquired a tip, and its color changed from green to bluish-pink. Meanwhile, the rest of the demon beret turned into a two-orbed sac. Tight, curly hairs commenced to sprout up.

Well, no need to mince words: this was a penis. And a pretty good-sized one at that. Indeed, for a moment, it covered the ceiling and ran down the walls of Bobby's cell!

Then the camera pulled back and the penis got smaller. Vague, human figures materialized. They were shrouded in steam but Bobby knew who they were: Jack was the owner of the penis. And Marilyn was attached to its head. Not all of her, of course—just her world-famous lips. She was servicing Jack in a bathtub. It was the large, sunken tub at the Lawford estate. A flashbulb kept popping in the background.

On the floor of his cell, Bobby Kennedy blushed. And wished for a less graphic scene.

For no reason he could think of, his wish was granted. The film left the orgy in the bathtub behind, and leaped through the steam to the future.

It was 1988 in Seattle. The reincarnated Bobby had just finished work, and he was walking to the Safeway to buy some groceries. His T-shirt was crusted with layers of sweat. He sniffed his left armpit. It stank. He sniffed again and made a face.

He was exhausted. He'd been working all day and part of the night on a big household move with lots of stairs. But he wasn't about to complain. At time-and-a-half he could save a few bucks, perhaps enough for a car by the fall. Special Ed had some junkers that ran pretty well. He'd told Bobby he'd give him a deal. And a car wasn't all Bobby needed: he could use some new clothes—a real nice set of duds—what with a woman in the picture for a change. His first girlfriend, in fact, since his untimely death.

Bobby thought about Loretta and he smiled. They were going on a date this coming weekend. They would meet for espresso, then stroll to the zoo. Maybe take in a movie. Maybe more.

Bobby entered the Safeway and grabbed a cart. He picked up the basics: macaroni and cheese, Smucker's jam, chopped pressed turkey, and bread. Plus Fritos for snacks. And Oreo cookies.

He'd never cooked in Life One; he'd never had to. And now, in Life Two, he hadn't bothered to learn because his shelf space in the rooming house was limited. And because all that he owned, in a culinary way, was one pot and two green plastic plates. And mostly because he hated to cook. Detested the act. Found it odious.

Still, Bobby thought, if Loretta dropped by, he ought to have something to offer. Something vaguely nutritious. Like carrots. Or celery sticks. Or better yet, plums. Plums were more romantic than carrots. But maybe, he thought, just a bit *too* romantic. Too juicy. Too luscious. Too sweet.

He wheeled his cart over to Produce. Which fruit would make the best impression? Bobby weighed the pros and cons of serving melon. On the plus side of the ledger, there was a hint of the erotic, something mildly suggestive and forbidden. It had to do with the structure, the hollow space deep inside. And those pulp-covered seeds in the center.

But would he spoil the effect with his plates? His olive-green cracked and chipped plastic plates? Moreover, with melon, you had to gamble on ripeness. What if he made the wrong call? What if he served her a limp, grainy slice on a hideous cracked and chipped plastic plate?

Too dicey, he thought. Too dicey. It was like running in the Oregon primary. He'd been crazy to enter that race. Without any ghettos, without any poor, without any rage, he had no base. So McCarthy had trounced him, a loss that cut deep. But that taught him a valuable lesson: *always* debate when you're down in the polls.

And never buy a melon if you're not sure.

Bobby moved on to the peaches. And shook his head at the price. It was outrageous. They cost over a dollar per pound!

But to their credit, he conceded, they were grown in California. California, Bobby thought. *California.* That's where he'd debated lazy Gene. And he'd cleaned the guy's clock, knocked his intellect out.

He had made some good friends in California. For example, young Cesar Chavez. Or was it old or dead Cesar now? Whatever the case, he had taken to Cesar. He remembered his dignified manner. He remembered a day when they talked about grapes.

And scurried over to the bin by the south wall. Perfect, he thought, the perfect fruit for Loretta! Juicy but unpretentious. A light and fun fruit he could serve without plates. And which fit his tight moving-man budget.

He put some green grapes in his cart. Then he walked to the long checkout line. Bobby looked at his grapes. He was one tired pup. But when he thought about Loretta, he was happy.

Until, that is, the line advanced to the candy, gum, and weekly tabloid section. Where Bobby glanced at a headline. And got depressed.

Now in fairness to the editors of the *National Enquirer*, Bobby couldn't get incensed about their story. I mean he could, but why bother? It was true! You probably remember the issue. It was the one claiming Lawford took pictures of Jack having oral sex with Marilyn in a bathtub.

Which didn't come as news to Bobby Kennedy. In fact he'd heard it more than twenty years before. During lunch with Edgar Hoover back at Justice. They used to meet once a month when Jack was president. And this meeting started off like the others. Which is to say, Edgar ranted at length: there were communists here and communists there; Martin King talked to Moscow every week; organized crime was a pinko-fag myth.

Bobby tried not to show his contempt. After all, he was dealing with a dangerous man. A *very* dangerous man, as things turned out. For at the end of the meal, Edgar sprung his surprise: a set of filthy, highly compromising snapshots. He pulled them out of his coat and went back to his pie—his second piece of pie—while Bobby gaped. "Those people are naked," Edgar said. He stuffed more pie in his mouth. "And they've been drinking. Note the bottle of scotch. Note the tits on that girl. Note the angle of your older brother's dong."

Edgar scraped his plate clean and licked off his fork. Then he put the photos back in his pocket. "Rest assured," he told Bobby, "the secret is safe. My people have the film in their possession."

"Five o'clock," Bobby said.

"Excuse me?" said Edgar.

"I want the negatives on my desk by five o'clock."

"With all due respect, the answer is no."

Bobby didn't press the issue, not directly. But when he finished his ice cream, he asked after Clyde. That was Edgar's companion, Clyde Tolson. "I'm concerned," Bobby said, "about your lovely wife's hemorrhoids. They must get frightfully itchy in this heat."

"You bastard!" said Edgar.

"You queer!" Bobby said.

"Those pictures are mine!" Edgar said.

"So?" Bobby said.

"I *own* you," Edgar said. "I have both of Jack's nuts in a vice."

"Could be," Bobby said. "But we know you're a homo."

"So what if I am?" Edgar said. "I'm not saying I am. But *if* I am."

"I would say," Bobby said, "we have your nuts in a vice."

It was a standoff, all right, an ugly standoff. And since the only move left was the boy-dog routine, they glowered at each other across the table. This went on for a while, until the waitress came by. "More coffee?" she inquired. "More tea?"

At last, Bobby broke off the stare. "Fucking Lawford," he muttered. "Fucking jerk."

Then he realized he was shopping at Safeway. He smiled so the people standing in line could see that he wasn't a loony.

And stopped smiling when he read the next headline. It was the one in *The Weekly World News*. The one that said Bobby had had Marilyn murdered. On Daddy's orders, no less. With Daddy's cash.

He grabbed a copy off the rack and started reading. He snapped the paper with irritation. So much malarkey!

According to the article Bobby made a special trip, flying out to California in late July. It said he'd boarded the plane with a sack full of green—a million dollars, in fact—to grease the wheels: to pay off the doctor, to pay off the cops, to pay off the L.A. county coroner.

Upon his arrival he'd been quite busy, wrote the reporter. He was "a ruthless blue-eyed rogue on rounds of death."

Bobby cursed and continued to read. His first stop, alleged the article, was Marilyn's shrink. He'd arranged for the doctor to prescribe the wrong pills, a lethal combination of barbituates. After that, he had bought off the cops. Their job was to locate her diaries; to find them and shred them into microscopic bits so the public wouldn't link her with the Kennedys. Finally, he'd purchased the coroner. The coroner's part was to make it look good, to make it look like booze and pills, no questions asked.

Well, this was too much: Bobby lost it. Right there in line, he flew off the handle. Became completely unhinged. Went bananas.

The poor lady behind him bore the brunt. He'd sensed her staring, with disapproval, in his direction. "You have a problem?" Bobby said to the lady. "You find my literary tastes to be substandard? Or is it merely that I'm all pitted out?"

The lady said nothing.

"Well *I've* got a problem." He waved the tabloid in her face. "Look at this! Where, in God's name, do they come up with this shit?"

Then he proceeded to explain how wrong they were. How his daddy, just for starters, had not set it up, had not set *anything* up, not since his stroke. About all he could do was drool, Bobby said, and he required an attendant to do that. He was a gibberish-spouting slobber machine who was as vital as an eggplant or a squash. So even if he'd wanted to have Marilyn whacked, heartless prick though Daddy was, he simply couldn't. Did the lady, Bobby asked, get that? Also, with regard to that bag of cold cash: out and out bullshit. Did she get that?

The lady said nothing.

Bobby shrugged. "It wasn't Hoover, if that's what you're thinking. That was never the problem, J. Edgar. See, he had our nuts. But we had his, too. Which was not, sad to say, the case with Hoffa. Oh we tried," Bobby said, "but his nuts wouldn't fit. He had a vice-immune pair. Know what I mean?"

The lady said nothing. And the lady looked scared.

"I understand. You don't know me from Adam. But I'm as harmless as an ant, believe me."

Bobby scrunched up his face to make it look like an ant's. He made two V's with his middle and index fingers. He placed the V's on his forehead. "See, an ant," Bobby said.

Bobby waggled his fingers.

He was deranged.

Not severely deranged like he became later on, when he tried to kill Carlos Marcello. But crazy enough to give anyone pause. For example, the lady in line. And the grocery clerk, who had pressed the red button—the hidden button beneath the counter—requesting help.

"Speaking of ants, which are a species of bug, that reminds me of something," Bobby said. "The woman had her telephone bugged. *Her own Goddamned phone.* Fucking *wired!*"

Even now, at this late date, it made him mad. Such a stupid, stupid blunder to have made! But then, when he recalled the awful quarrel they'd had, Bobby's anger gave way to remorse.

He remembered the scene in her apartment: him screaming at Marilyn, shouting "Where the fuck is it?" as he attempted to disassemble the mouthpiece. Over and over, shouting "Where the fuck is it?" while Marilyn cowered, stinking drunk, beside her bed. Puke, stinking drunk at ten-thirty in the morning. On her knees beside her bed, as if in prayer. She was clutching a bottle of white sleeping pills. It was August and hot as blazes. But she kept shivering.

Bobby looked away from the lady. He looked away from the carts and the people in line, out to the Health and Beauty aisle of the Safeway. "Jimmy Hoffa bugged her bug," he said at last. "He put a tap on her tap. You understand? He had the *goods*," Bobby said. "He had our nuts in a vice. She was screwing up the whole shebang!"

He jabbed his finger at his *Weekly World News*. "We

had the motive, that's for sure," Bobby said. "But I did *not* have the woman taken out. I loved her," he said. "Just like I loved Oriet. And I admit I offed my goldfish with a flashlight. But once was enough; I wouldn't do it again."

Suddenly, the lady looked relieved.

From the floor of his cell Bobby Kennedy watched as the manager came to her rescue. He saw the grocery clerk make the cuckoo sign and then finger the cuckoo: Bobby. The manager nodded. He had seen many cuckoos. He beckoned Bobby aside. Bobby followed.

"What seems to be the problem?" asked the manager.

"*The* problem?" said Bobby. "*The* problem?"

"Something wrong with the question?" asked the manager.

"Well it's kind of naive," Bobby said.

"Why's that?" asked the manager.

"Use your head!" Bobby said. "There were *hundreds* of problems to deal with! Cuba. Berlin. The U.S. Steel crisis. Hell, there were thousands. Take Laos.

"But let's say you forced me. Say I *had* to pick one. Pertaining to Marilyn, I mean. In that case I'd point to the ramifications. The *very serious* ramifications, I might add. As I was explaining to the nice lady there..."

Bobby covered his mouth with his hand. Then he lowered his voice. And spoke frankly. "Just imagine how it was from our end. If Marilyn talked—like she'd threatened to do—you could kiss Jack good-bye. Impeached! And if Jack gets impeached that means *I* get impeached, so you can kiss the Hoffa probe good-bye. And ditto," Bobby added, "for civil rights. Because Lyndon, fucking Lyndon..."

He shook his head. "You'll have to excuse my language. It comes from being resurrected as a moving man. 'Fucking this,' 'fucking that,' 'fucking fuck,' all day long. Not that I'm complaining," Bobby said. "I work with a great bunch of guys. Guys as good, in their way, as my staff back at Justice. And even the *Times* gave me that. The fucking *New York Times*..."

He smiled ruefully. "Those bastards never liked me. Couldn't *stand* me. But they did say I had a fine staff: loyal, effective, pragmatic, and tough. Which is precisely how I feel about the guys. Or at least about some of the guys. Full-Time John, for example, is tough. And Special Ed is quite effective when he's sober. Although, just between us, he's lazy. Especially at the end of the day. I'm *always* the one who folds up the pads. And I always clean the truck, which is a drag.

"But getting back to LBJ and civil rights. I know, I

know: the Civil Rights Act. That's what you're thinking, the Act. I imply he's a racist, yet *he* gets it passed. So who am I to find fault?"

Bobby shrugged. "They say hindsight is perfect," he said.

"Look—" said the manager.

"No need for concern. I'll pay for the food, don't worry. I'll be happy—in fact, *delighted*—to pay. For the grapes, in particular," Bobby said.

"But one final note regarding Lyndon. How could we know, before Johnny got whacked, that the cowboy would change his tune? Ever hear the guy talk about Mexicans? Ever listen to him cuss in his office? In the fucking *Oval Office?* He was *crude.* He *defiled* that office. He—"

"Young man—" said the manager.

"Young man my ass!" Bobby said. "I'm older than you are. By far. I was born—" he began.

But then the film picked up speed. And the sound track shut off. And the color flattened.

Yes, the movie had turned old-fashioned once more: herky-jerky, black and white, and oddly silent. The characters gestured at a high rate of speed: crossing arms, pointing fingers, and shrugging shoulders; slamming fists into palms, nodding yes, nodding no.

Bobby watched the ridiculous scene. And remembered what he'd said to the manager. No, there wasn't any need to call the police. Yes, he promised to clean up his language. And he'd pay for the groceries. And never shop there again.

He was a little stressed out, that's all. From working O.T. so he could buy a used car from Special Ed who was this wild guy he worked with. From his upcoming date with Loretta the fox. (He hadn't had a relationship in twenty years.) And mostly from being returned from the dead, which is a highly stressful life change as those things go. Right up there, he'd wager, with marriage, divorce, getting cancer, and winning the lottery.

Not that he hadn't deserved the rebirth. He was long past denial, he assured the manager. He'd cheated on Ethel, his kid had OD'd, and he'd thrown a horrid tantrum while Marilyn cowered. He had scared her to death, in a literal sense, since her suicide occurred just hours later. Oh, he hadn't *intended* to get angry. He'd set out to persuade her to go to a clinic, to go to some ranch for a cure. And to stop making threats about calling the press so she could spill all the beans and ruin everything.

But he hadn't convinced her, which is why he got mad, although he really couldn't blame her in a way.

People didn't go to clinics in those days. And if they did, they didn't flaunt it. They had pride.

Now, of course, things were different. Now they had the Betty Ford Center. Now, to stay famous, you had to get hooked, then write a book about recovery once you were clean. It was a fucking badge of honor, for Christ's sake!

But who the hell was Betty Ford in '62? Or *Jerry* Ford, for that matter? Goofy Jerry. He used to *eat* guys like Jerry for lunch.

Still, no need for concern: he'd pay for the grapes. And for the libelous rag. And all the rest.

Bobby watched himself exit the store. He watched himself trudge up the hill. As he crossed Twenty-third he pondered his future: he was no longer welcome at Safeway. Which would mean, from now on, he'd have to shop at Larry's Market. A warning flickered: *higher prices, higher prices.*

He switched his grip on the grocery bag. And kept walking, for twenty minutes, to the rooming house. He unloaded his bag in the kitchen. Then he climbed up the stairs and collapsed on his bed. "I'll take a shower in a minute," Bobby thought.

But he didn't make a move in that direction. He just

lay there and let his mind drift. How long, Bobby wondered, did it take grapes to shrivel? And why had he been such an asshole? After leaving poor Marilyn in a state of pure terror, he'd driven over to Peter Lawford's for a swim. "I was such a royal asshole," Bobby thought.

He tried to put his mind elsewhere.

He thought of work.

Where would they send him tomorrow, he mused. Perhaps to some fancy law firm. Perhaps to deliver a chair. An overstuffed chair, he imagined. An overstuffed chair worth three to five grand for some fat, wealthy client to plunk his ass on. *Five grand for a chair for a fatso*, he thought. Instead of spending it on worthy social programs.

But then again, there were hardly any social programs left. Besides, who was he to pass judgment? Who was he, indeed? Just some low-life. Just some low-life who lived in a pukey rented room with a pukey olive carpet on the floor. In a house full of druggies on the wrong side of town.

And he deserved it, did he ever. He had earned it! Not by screwing around—lots of people did that. Not by losing his temper in front of Marilyn. Not even by experiencing, in the wake of her death—when, miraculously, no scandal emerged—a degree of relief that compared with his grief. An unseemly response. But understandable.

No, what made him so loathsome was that one afternoon, as he'd lounged by a pool with Peter Lawford—believing that Marilyn would go to the press, convinced that Jack's presidency was in peril—he had told Peter Lawford that he should've killed the bitch. He should've whacked the mouthy cunt in her apartment. He said he truly regretted having wasted the chance. He said he wished he'd had the balls.

And he had meant it.

The camera pulled back from the figure on the bed. And returned to the office at Justice. Bobby's opulent, majestic, power office. No dearth of costly furniture in here!

The sound track came on. The colors blazed forth. There were the deep reds and blues of the flag. And the rich, oiled browns of the handsome oak desk. And, of course, the fucking green of the beret.

Bobby sighed as the camera zoomed in. "Here we go again," he thought.

Sure enough, the green beret began to change. But this time, thank God, at least it wasn't going phallic. If anything, the opposite was happening. Which is to say, the green beret was developing holes. Four holes, to be exact. Two on the sides. Plus a hole on the top and one more on the bottom. The bottom hole was wider than the others.

This made Bobby glad, very glad. He had had it up to here with Jack's pecker. It was such an irksome pecker. It was incorrigible! Whatever came next was *bound* to be better. No matter what the episode, it would be better.

Or so he told himself.

But he was wrong.

What came next was much worse than an impolitic prick. What came next was a laboratory coat.

It seems the fucking beret was no longer green. It was as white—well—as a laboratory coat. Which is what, in point of fact, it had become. And standing inside it was a man. The man had a head, two arms, and two legs. They stuck out of the holes in the coat.

Needless to say, this was the scientist again. He appeared to be pleased with himself. He was humming a ditty as he strolled through his lab. He had worked out the kinks in his napalm. He had added polystyrene to make it stick to the skin. And Willie Peter, as those flyboys liked to call it. A stroke of genius, white phosphorus, which made it burn to the bone.

The mad scientist beamed. He rubbed his hands. He

was due for a medal. He was due for a raise. The product had been tested in the field. And it got the job done, cooked the gooks to perfection. There was certainly no need for further testing.

But even so, late at night, he liked to test it again. Just as a painter liked to gaze at his best paintings. Just as a writer liked to thumb through his most cherished books. Just as a mother liked to view her sleeping baby.

With love, thought the scientist. I'm in love with my baby. I'm in lovey-dovey love, foolish love.

He continued to beam as he strolled through the lab, past the carcasses of charred human specimens. Tiny charred human specimens.

The madman chuckled. He was laughing about a joke he'd made up, a funny name he'd thought up for his specimens. They were his "Rice-Eating Crispies." He was so clever! His product was flawless, his mission complete.

He chuckled to himself as he walked. He chuckled all the way to the back of the lab.

Where he came upon two cages.

And laughed maniacally.

From his perch on the floor, Bobby Kennedy groaned. "Jesus Christ, no," he said.

He was expecting to see a bunch of babies. A bunch of hungry, filthy, squalling Asian babies. But, boy, was he in for a surprise. This time the cages held grown-up caucasians They held a man and a woman, respectively.

Bobby stared at the woman in the movie. He stared at the woman in the cage. She was a frightened platinum blonde. She was a naked platinum blonde. She was a blonde in distress. She was Marilyn! Her eyes were red-rimmed and her hair was in tangles. "Call Joe DiMaggio!" she kept pleading.

And Bobby would've if he could've. But he couldn't. All he could do was remember a day when he and Marilyn had gone for a walk. Just an innocent walk down Fifth Avenue. Although it didn't *feel* innocent to Bobby. It felt scary and big, as if something might happen.

This was back before the shit hit the fan. Back, for that matter, before he broke his marriage vows. This was their first official date, his and Marilyn's.

Oh, they'd met once before, but that wasn't on purpose. The meeting occurred in late May. At an event where she sang for Jack's birthday. And where she and Bobby played a bit of footsie backstage.

But that didn't count; they were drunk. This second meeting, however, did count. It was October in New

York City in '61. She was shooting a film in Manhattan. And he was up there on government business. So he called on an impulse and suggested a walk.

The weather was perfect for a walk. He remembered the crisp autumn air. And he remembered, as well, a strange story she told, about being locked up in a cell. A padded cell for psychotics in a hospital. They had stripped off her clothes and thrown her inside. And after doing that, they'd come to gawk. She was, after all, a screen goddess. So on breaks and at lunch they had crowded the hall: the orderlies, the nurses, and, yes, the doctors. They had stared through the window. They made faces. They waved. They brought their colleagues down from other floors. This went on for three days until someone called Joe, her ex-husband Joe, who retrieved her.

Marilyn clutched Bobby's arm as she spoke. "I went in for depression," she said. "I went in for a rest, nothing more."

Bobby found himself moved by her story. Deeply moved, and, reluctant though he was to admit it, aroused by her plight inside the ward. Naked, held captive. He would've looked, too.

He felt the grip of her fingers on his arm. He felt a thrill in his bones. He felt a lot.

He wanted to tell Marilyn about his fish, Oriet. And

about waiting on the steps when he was four. And many other things he'd never mentioned to his wife. Or to anyone on earth, come to think of it.

He caught a whiff of her scent and his heart jumped a mile.

He understood that he was headed for big trouble.

The camera pulled back from the woman in her cage, and focused on the man in his cage. He was a sandy-haired man with blue eyes and no clothes. He was Robert F. Kennedy in the buff!

But in a way he wasn't Bobby, although he was. I mean he didn't seem ruthless, world-famous, all that. Nude persons in cages rarely do. He looked pale and scared. Defeated. Unmanned.

The mad scientist cackled and leered. Then he reached for a bottle on top of the cage—a spray bottle marked NAPALM—and sprayed.

The Bobby Kennedy on the ceiling started writhing.

And the Bobby Kennedy in the cell, who was observing himself, felt a burning sensation in his arm. In his upper left forearm.

Which was absurd. He was watching a movie. *This was pretend.*

But even so, it was a penetrating burn. It was a

penetrating bone-burning burn. He heard his flesh start to sizzle. He saw white flames shooting out. He felt his arm go all gooey.

Bobby screamed.

Or at least he thought he screamed.

He didn't really.

It was more of a chirp than a scream. The sort of chirp that a baby bird makes. That a half-dead baby bird tends to make. That a delirious half-dead convict-scum baby bird tends to make as he's breathing his last.

It didn't even register on Gerbil's monitor. Gerbil didn't hear a chirp or a scream. All he noticed was that Bobby was brushing his arm, his upper-left forearm, with his hand. It was kind of a slow-motion swat.

Bobby swatted several times and then he stopped. He rested his arms by his side. His gaunt, dirty face assumed a peaceful expression.

What the fuck is going on here, Gerbil thought.

THREE

Within a week, Bobby Kennedy turned up at the shop. At seven forty-five on a Monday morning. He told Jake he was broke, that he needed a job.

Jake regarded his ex-employee with suspicion. How the hell did he bust out, Jake was thinking. I better call the cops, Jake was thinking. But he might have a gun—

"I don't," Bobby said.

"Excuse me?"

"No gun," Bobby said.

"How did you know—"

Bobby smiled at Jake. And gazed into Jake's eyes.

He was using magic. He was blurring Jake's memories of certain events. He was making Jake forget he was a fugitive. So that Jake would agree to give him a job and pair him with that fellow they'd just hired. You know who I mean, that cowboy poet from Montana. The drifter with the great line of shit.

Bobby worked with the guy for three days. Bobby told his whole story to the guy. He even performed a small miracle or two, just enough to pique the cowboy's curiosity.

After which Bobby vanished, truly vanished for good.

Or so it's asserted by the moving men.

But getting back to that scene in Jake's office: Bobby Kennedy was blurring Jake's memory, as I say. It was simpler than explaining what had happened.

To be sure, Bobby could've explained. He could've told Jake about Gerbil the guard, and how he'd foiled Gerbil's plan to make him crazy.

The way he'd done it was by going crazy first. By going stark, raving mad from all those movies he'd seen. By going over the edge from his shame.

So when Gerbil commenced to string Bobby along by shouting through the slot in Bobby's door, he found that Bobby was immune to his false promises. And false promises formed the heart of Gerbil's program. He'd promise freedom one day and not grant it the next; promise creamy chocolate ice cream and not deliver; promise Bobby a shower that Bobby never got to take.

It was a trick Gerbil had learned back in guard school. How to do a thorough mindfuck on a guy. And it usually worked in a hurry. A few days on average. A week at the most.

But you can't break a mind if it's broken. So Bobby

just lay there, catatonic, removed. Too far gone to be suckered. Beyond pain. Waiting, simply waiting, for the death he deserved.

While Gerbil got madder and madder. Mad enough, maybe, to storm into the cell and slash Bobby's throat.

After raping him.

But then, of all things, the Movie Gods intervened. Yes, at last the Movie Gods were acting mercifully. They weren't showing a film about mistreating Marilyn. Or about Bobby the ruthless young pol. Or pet-goldfish trauma. Or Jack's errant prick. Or fried Asian babies.

And the lot.

Instead they were trying a bold new approach. An approach devoid of Kennedys and their problems. They were holding a festival of Three Stooges flicks. Quality Stooges, in fact. All Curlys.

They started off with the famous boxing episode. That's the one in which the melody to "Pop Goes the Weasel" causes Curly to become a ferocious prize fighter.

This was followed by the feather-pie episode.

Which was followed by the one in which the Stooges take a cab from New York City to the Nile and find King Tut.

Which was followed by the timeless "Doctor Howard,

Doctor Fine," and several classics involving Limburger cheese.

Now there's no telling which of Curly's "Wu-wu-wu-wu's" caused the zombie on the cell floor to wake up. Or even if it was the "wu-wu-wu's." Conceivably it was the "Biddyboo" song. Or Larry's penchant for eating pancakes doused with catsup. It's even possible, some might theorize, that the catalytic event was as subtle as a single "Nyuk-nyuk-nyuk." Or Curly's method for making the soup of the day, which was to pour a pot of water through a rubber chicken.

But all this is idle speculation. What can't be disputed is the smile. Yes, goldfish killer though he was, Bobby smiled. Heartless lover though he'd been, Bobby smiled. Belly-poker, war-maker, failed newsboy, convict scum—for fucking once he let it go.

And simply smiled.

Which stopped Gerbil in his homicidal tracks. He suspended his wrath out of sheer amazement. Things just didn't add up, didn't square. The naked man on the monitor who was all skin and bones, who was too weak to pick at his scabs, who didn't have the energy to wave off the rats, had suddenly started to smile. And not only to smile, but to laugh. To point at the ceiling and cackle and snort. To apparently be having a blast.

Gerbil's reading of the situation was correct. Bobby Kennedy was having a fine old time, fueled, in part, by the alum episode. That's the one in which Curly adds some alum to the stew, thereby causing Moe and Larry to develop lockjaw. By the end of the film they're blowing bubbles as they breathe.

This was followed by the parrot debacle. It begins when the parrot flies out of its cage and into the Thanksgiving turkey. Logically enough, this results in a turkey that squawks as it hops on its platter, and eventually flies the length of the table as the Stooges and the guests run for their lives.

Bobby rolled around and smacked the floor in hysterics. When he came to himself, he saw more guests. Only these guests weren't actors like in the Stooges. These were actual, real-life guests. They were guests of his and Ethel's at Hickory Hill, at a party for the French ambassador.

One of the guests was Arthur Schlesinger. He was wearing his trademark bow tie. And he was smoking a fat cigar. Which he managed to keep above water and lit when Ethel pushed him in the pool with all his clothes on.

Good old Arthur, Bobby thought. Good old Arthur.

And there was Brumus, Bobby's oaf of a dog. Ambling over to the stodgy ambassador and taking a piss on his leg.

Bobby watched himself scoot out of sight. He watched himself hide in the pantry. He watched himself laughing so hard that he cried.

He understood what the Movie Gods were up to. They were airing goofy footage from his past. They were giving Bobby glimpses of his Three Stooges side, a way of looking at his life without despairing.

They showed that weird poet guy, for example. What was his name? Allen Ginstein? Ginstein, Ginsburg. The nut with the beard. Chanting "oms" on the floor by Bobby's desk. On the floor chanting oms after meeting with Bobby to lobby against the war.

Too much, Bobby thought. Absurd. Emitting strange hippie sounds from the lotus position. Commandeering a senator's office!

Bobby gazed at the fellow and chuckled. He had a feeling the Three Stooges would approve. And that Jesus Christ himself might well approve.

He could hear Curly's voice going "wu-wu-wu-wu."

He felt love for this fool of a poet.

The Movie Gods were pleased with Bobby's

progress. So much so that they started to introduce
scenes that addressed a less frivolous theme: Bobby
Kennedy's capacity for doing good works. Bobby
Kennedy's quiet decency.

Not the great public moments recorded by history—
his cool head on Cuba, all that—but the little stuff that
hardly got noticed. Like using his magic, when he returned for Life Two, to patch up the dings in the walls. To
protect careless partners who scraped the paint with
their hand trucks. And who never even knew it, thanks
to Bobby.

Or causing a string of sequential green lights—an
unheard of event in Seattle traffic—in order to help a
nervous new driver who was afraid of rolling back while
doing hill starts.

Or causing a string of sequential red lights if a partner
was ill or hung over, in order to give the ailing partner
more time to gather up steam for the next load.

Or let's say he was paired with Special Ed. And that
he used his magic powers to determine, in advance, that
a customer was high-strung and litigious. You know
the type—they're so common these days—flag-waving
vermin who love to tattle. The type who'd like nothing
better than an excuse to call Jake and make a stink about
that wise guy, Special Ed. Who might threaten to sue

unless Jake fired Ed.

Well, then Bobby might take preventive action. Such as reaching inside of Special Ed's mind to temporarily subdue his reckless impulses. Thereby depriving himself of Ed's wit, of his outrageous remarks and wild stories. Of Ed's aforementioned and practically singular knack for making Bobby's burdens disappear.

Yet Bobby was happy to pay that small price if he could keep a moving colleague out of trouble. He was always sticking up for his close friends.

Take the day Full-Time John went to the church. It was a very big church, Seattle's largest cathedral, where he'd gone to deliver a rostrum.

Well, that church did a number on John. He returned to the shop filled with awe. He couldn't believe the stained glass. And the intricate paintings. The sheer size of the place.

He described what he'd seen to the others. "There were angels on the ceiling," he explained. "Angels and cherubs with wings and shit!"

Which caused Andy, the kid from college, to almost snicker. Andy the snob who was working for the summer, whose contempt for John's rusticity had been aroused.

But Bobby stopped the snicker with a glower. He shot

Andy a look—the kind he used to give Hoffa—that shut the little college fucker's scornful trap.

Not to mention the things Bobby did in Life One, such as showing up when Jackie miscarried. Being there, by her side, while Jack was off wenching.

Or holding sore-infested babies in the South. Babies so dirty, repulsive, and sick that the SNCC workers themselves wouldn't touch them. And the amazing part is he didn't do it to impress. He didn't do it for the votes; he *had* these votes. Bobby did it because the filthy babies needed holding.

Well, you get the idea: he had some good points. Indeed, if the Movie Gods had titled this segment, it would've gone something like this: ROBERT F. KENNEDY'S NON-SCUMBAG SIDE.

But the Gods didn't bother with a title. They just slowly closed the curtains on the scene. And then the curtains themselves dematerialized. The house lights went on. Which is to say the one light—the mesh-covered bulb on Bobby's ceiling.

Bobby stared at the ugly ceiling. And at the shit—his own shit—in a corner. And at a rat crawling by. A real flesh-and-blood rat.

Bobby felt like shaking hands with the rat. Even

Well, maybe he'd pass on the kiss. But he felt pretty good, all in all. The long movie from hell was really over. And he'd sat through the whole fucking thing. Every act, every word, every last bitter frame.

He'd faced up to his defects like a man. Or at least to a few of his flaws. And he'd discovered his virtues. Or at least one or two. The point is, he was healed. Sort of healed. He was as healed, at any rate, as he would be in this life.

He felt ready, truly ready, to die. And if dying was not what the gods had in store, what he craved, above all, was some french fries. Yes, a Big Mac and fries. With, maybe, a shake.

Bobby thought about chocolate milkshakes. And lo and behold a milkshake appeared!

Bobby gaped. He just couldn't believe it. But there it was in his hand—a cool, waxy cup.

Bobby's head was filled with tingles like in the old days. Plus blue-and-white spirals and Oriet's voice and mournful sax riffs—in short, the magic.

Bobby's magic was back.

Or was he dreaming?

There was only one way to find out. If the magic was real then the milkshake was real. So he sat up and lifted the cup. He put the cup to his lips.

He tasted chocolate!

Bobby drank the shake down in one gulp. Which gave him a headache of show-stopping caliber. The type you get from eating ice cream. Killer headache.

But so what, Bobby thought. Big deal. The important thing was that it tasted just fine.

Bobby waited for the headache to blow over. Then he crumpled the empty cup. It felt great to have the strength to crumple cups.

Bobby sat there contentedly squeezing away, surveying the cell as he crumpled. Soon he spotted the large, ugly rat. Only now he didn't want to shake its hand. What he wanted was to kill it. Or to maim it. To at least show the rat who was boss of the cell.

Bobby crumpled the cup even tighter. Then he reared back, took aim, and fired.

He missed the rat by a good two feet.

Bobby laughed. "I'm kind of rusty," he explained.

But the rat was not amused in the least. It stood up on its two hind legs. It growled at Bobby in its ferocious rat way.

Bobby smiled at the large, ugly rat. He gazed into its eyes. He was using magic. He was causing the rat to turn into a kitten.

"Here kitty, kitty," Bobby said.

The sweetest kitten in the world walked up to Bobby. It climbed into his lap. It started purring.

"Pretty kitty," Bobby cooed. "Pretty kitty." Bobby petted the kitty. She was soft. He closed his eyes and stroked her fur.

He was happy. He was as happy, he realized, as he'd ever been in either life. He was deliriously, pig-in-shit happy.

Speaking of which, he smelled shit.

Bobby opened his eyes and stared at the corner. There it was: his big pile of shit.

It took some effort but Bobby smiled at the shit. Then he gazed at the shit in that new way of his.

And turned it into a vase full of sweet peas. Bobby savored the pleasant aroma. And he feasted his eyes on the colors: pale blues, soft pinks, an array of pastels.

"See the flowers?" Bobby said to the kitty.

The kitty nuzzled Bobby's hand.

The kitty purred.

Bobby decided to make some more flowers. In fact, he went a little crazy on the flowers.

Not that making roses was excessive. And who could begrudge him several dahlias? After twenty-three days in solitary confinement, you'd crave yellow dahlias, too. But when he put in a row of white gladiolas and a wall full of lavender foxgloves, it didn't exactly add to the decor. And by the time he'd introduced the African violets, the cactus, the jade tree, and the orchids—not to mention the seventeen orange nasturtiums—well, aesthetically speaking, it stank.

Now in fairness to Bobby, he'd never been known for sensitivity to aesthetic concerns. The fight for justice, not beauty, had been his strong suit. A minor example of how he *didn't* mix the two was that he used to wear tacky white socks. White socks with black shoes on the job. The nation's number-one lawman, no less. Prosecuting Hoffa in footwear like that! Until Ethel made him switch to navy blue.

But that was a long time ago. Now he didn't have any socks. Now he didn't have a stitch of clothing to his name. Or any sense of where to go or what to do.

Oh, it was fun to make milkshakes and flowers. Sort of fun. Mild fun. Okay fun.

Actually, it wasn't all that fun.

It sure was nice being happy, Bobby thought. Then he shrugged a little bitterly and thought, "Fuck happy."

FOUR

As Bobby stood in Jake's office he could've told him all this. And about what happened next, which was unusual.

It began when the kitten popped out of his lap, and started poking around the garden. Soon she was lost among the gladiola stems.

Bobby sighed and lay back on the floor. He stared at the mesh-covered bulb. He gazed at the bulb in that strange, special way.

And turned it into a chandelier.

Much better, Bobby thought. Much improved.

He dimmed the lights on the new chandelier. The little cat mewed as she flitted in and out of the seventeen orange nasturtiums.

Bobby closed his eyes and slowed his breathing. He listened for Oriet's voice. He listened for the mournful saxophone riffs. Then he focused his attention on the prison.

He heard shouting and clanging on the surface. And just below that, the unspoken emotions: ache and despair in abundance. Anger, self-pity, and six kinds of hate. Or was it twelve or twenty-four?

It was a lot.

Bobby used his magic powers to delve deeper. And what he sensed, at the core, was self-loathing. Wherever he reached—the chow hall, the yard, even the guards in their towers—he was encountering souls who detested themselves.

I can relate, Bobby thought.

He locked into some malice nearby. He followed the trail through the slot in the door. He followed with his mind to Gerbil's station.

Yes, there he was in all his splendor: fucking Gerbil. Fat fucking Gerbil with crumbs in his lap. He'd been eating another corndog. And he was pretty well convinced that it was laced. How else could he explain what he was seeing on the monitor? Fucking flowers and fucking kittens and crumpled cups!

Bobby probed Gerbil's mind even further. He discovered what Gerbil had done. And all the things that his keeper had *wanted* to do.

It was a long goddamned list of vile deeds. And when the list was complete, a fish appeared in Bobby's head. It was a young, pretty goldfish. It was Oriet.

She flashed Bobby a wink, then turned into a shark.

She showed Bobby her teeth.

She swam away.

Bobby sat up abruptly. His eyes were blazing. He had a reason for living at last. He had a mission that compared with nailing Hoffa. Or with chasing down and whipping Hubert's ass. Or with siccing the IRS on Roy Cohn.

He couldn't wait to get started on his revenge.

Which, in and of itself, was kind of dull. I mean here was a guy with the Kennedy smarts and genuine Kennedy magic, pitted against a dumb-as-dirt foe.

You couldn't even call it a contest. So there's no need to bore you with an account of Bobby's tricks. How he walked through impenetrable walls. Or how he gave himself a shave without a razor. How he flew and cast spells and affected the weather by making it rain puppies on the yard. Cute beagle pups for the convicts to pat.

But I'm getting ahead of myself. Suffice it to say that by the following morning, the prison was in an uproar. There was the matter of Inmate Kennedy, to begin with. Gone. Disappeared. And all his records as well. Every copy of every file about his case. And every duplicate copy of every file. Even the newspaper clippings about the case.

It was as if he had never existed. And ditto for Bobby's friend, Noodle. Noodle, who'd shown him the ropes in the joint. Disappeared and never heard from again.

It's asserted by some that Bobby spirited him away to a small town in western Pennsylvania. They say he works afternoons in a video store, and continues to play a mean banjo.

But to return to Mister Foley: he was in a jam. That was Gerbil's real name, Clarence Foley. And he had some explaining to do. Not that his superiors believed, for a second, that Gerbil was the author of this disaster. They were completely in the dark as to the cause. They were frazzled and angry. They were *scared*.

But even so, there was a reason why they were bosses: these men were shrewd judges of character. They understood that Mister Foley was a moron. A vicious prick, to be sure, the type they liked to have around. But subtlety was not the numbskull's strong suit.

He simply lacked the imagination to place flowers in a cell. Or the kindness to loose puppies in the yard. Thereby affording the convicts a chance to cuddle something soft and responsive. To give and get love. To forget where they were. To forget *who* they were.

If only briefly.

Well, it just wasn't Gerbil's style: an act of kindness. And this business of erasing every trace of Inmate Kennedy and every trace of Inmate Noodle. *Every trace.* An impossible feat that could not be performed. And certainly not by a dimwit.

Yes, stupidity had served Gerbil well. But not well enough to account for the pose in which he was found the next morning. Asleep in his chair with a bottle of wine— an empty bottle of Ripple—on the floor. With his pants and his underpants scrunched by his ankles. With his cum-covered wang in his hand. And Bobby Kennedy's final touch—a truly dazzling flourish—the magazine that was draped over Gerbil's thigh. The one filled with pictures of naked young boys.

Bobby had a real flair for this shit. Take the matter of the record erasure. Changing history like that. It was impressive.

Yet as any knowledgeable sorcerer would be quick to point out, he'd acquired sufficient powers to go further. With one minor spell he could've caused the higher-ups to forget he'd been inside their rotten joint. In fact, that's just what he did for old Noodle: by the end of the week no bureaucrat cared or even knew about Noodle's escape. A kind of prophylactic brainwash, so to speak.

For Bobby's own part, however, he chose to linger in their minds, a solid memory without a single paper trail. Which, over the years, would fill the bastards with doubt, would gnaw away at their dreams, might keep them humble.

And then there were Bobby's broad brushstrokes. Like what he did to the food-service guys. At least to a few of the guys. To those mean, hardass cons who spit and pissed in the food that they served to the child molesters.

Well, suddenly these bulldogs were eating that food, the scrambled eggs they'd just fouled. They couldn't help it. They ate and they retched, ate some more as they gagged.

And never spit or pissed in food from that day on.

It was a neat piece of work.

As were the puppies.

He set them loose after breakfast. Countless beagles.

Bobby watched from his perch by the concertina wire as the sweetest chaos in the world ensued. As the convicts broke ranks to cuddle the dogs while the guards shouted orders that no one listened to.

He had made himself invisible, of course.

He enjoyed a good laugh.
He had earned it.
Then he launched himself up. He ascended in spirals.
He heard the sound of yapping beagles far below.

FIVE

And there is even more to tell, so legend has it. It is said, for example, that after Bobby left the joint, he pulled a post-hypnotic stunt in the chow hall. It involved bologna stew as you might guess. It seems the stew underwent a transformation. One minute it was stew; the next minute it wasn't. It had become a classic Cape Cod summer feed. There were trays full of sweet August corn. And buckets of clams. And fresh lobster tails. And countless bowls of warm, melted butter.

Such a thing had never happened in the joint. Nor had the eventuality been anticipated. Hence there wasn't a policy on what to do when prison food turns into different, better food by dint of magic, and the guards had no choice but to let the cons feast the way that rich people feast.

Or so it's said.

And it's said that Bobby Kennedy turned up in Las Vegas after spiraling over the walls. He had a craving, rumor has it, for neon and glitz.

Bobby ate a lot of burgers down there. Lots and lots

of greasy burgers and greasy fries. And rich chocolate shakes. He couldn't seem to eat enough, although he did take time out to get laid. Or "get his nuts out of hock" as the cons aptly put it when a fellow's had no pussy for a while.

Bobby's date was a waitress at Caesar's Palace. She wore a cute little toga. Her name was Suzy. Or so she's described in almost every account of Bobby Kennedy's adventures in Las Vegas. It's said he gambled, chased skirts, and was often seen by the slots, steering widows on fixed incomes to the hot ones. And if a slot wasn't hot, Bobby Kennedy *made* it hot: the percentage of jackpot payoffs rose dramatically.

And that wasn't all that took place. Something stranger yet occurred in the casino. It happened at a crowded roulette wheel. Bobby Kennedy was staring in that new, special way, gazing into the minds of the players, then looking over at the wheel and causing wins for those bettors who worked for companies that didn't offer health insurance. And for young couples with kids who dreamed of owning a home. And for some old folks who had marched for civil rights.

In short, he was enjoying a bit of bleeding-heart fun when the amazing thing occurred: a man came over. Or what appeared to be a man, at any rate. And a very well-dressed one at that. His Brooks Brothers suit was a conservative gray. His monogrammed shirt was made of silk. He had cuff links of gold and a silver-tipped cane.

"You can do anything you want," he said to Bobby.

"Excuse me?" said Bobby.

"You have the magic!" he said, as he stroked his Vandyke beard with his long, thin fingers. "The world is your oyster. Just think! You can visit your grandkids and bring them new toys. Or talk to Teddy and make him clean up his act. Or whack Marcello's whole family and do it *right* for a change. Or set Loretta Easton straight on the First Amendment!"

Bobby stared at the speaker.

And burst out laughing.

Whereupon the unctuous fellow became unmasked. Once he realized his quarry had a nearly pure heart, that Bobby Kennedy had been cleansed beyond fear, beyond ambition and the desire to dominate others, beyond *all* sinful predilections except for screwing, the creature's custom-made Italian shoes disintegrated. A pair of webbed demon's feet took their place. And a hairless red tail snaked its way through his suit as prongs emerged on the tip of his cane.

"You lose," Bobby said. "And you could really use a bath."

It was true: the devil's envoy smelled quite rank.

Bobby shrugged and wandered over to play craps. He lost a few chips on the "Don't Pass" line, but recouped with a series of place bets. He won four in a row at seven to six.

Then he started to converse with a beam of light. Or so it's purported in the accounts. It's alleged that Bobby Kennedy stepped back from the table and held a heated discussion with the light.

"Not yet," Bobby said. He put his hands on his hips. He said, "I want to see Yosemite before I go." He said, "Of *course* I know it's winter. Do I look stupid?"

A lonely and desperate young man shuffled past. Bobby handed all his winnings to the guy.

"For me?" the man said.

"For you," Bobby said. "Just enough to buy a ticket back to Denver."

"How did you know—"

"Don't piss it away. Just get on the bus," Bobby said. "Juliet wants you back."

"She does?" the man said.

Bobby nodded. "She needs you home. She's pregnant."

"My wife?" the man said.

"Four months," Bobby said.

"Are you sure?"

"It's a girl," Bobby said.

The young man scurried off to cash in his chips.

Bobby sighed and turned back to the light. "Okay, bag Yosemite," he said. "But give me a week on the trucks."

The light flickered red.

"Then three days," Bobby said. "Your people put me through the wringer. I think they owe me."

The light wavered briefly before it turned a friendly blue.

Bobby smiled and went off to find Suzy. He bought a scotch and told Suzy he'd just talked to a fish, a tall goldfish with wings named Oriet. He said the fish had tried to get him to go to heaven. But that he, Bobby Kennedy, the *reincarnated* Bobby Kennedy, had demanded a short visit up north. "I want to see my old pals," he explained.

"You're crazy," she said.

"I still have time for a quickie."

"I get off in ten minutes," Suzy said.

Or so it's avowed by some of Bobby's disciples, although there's little hard corroborative evidence. Conceivably, the whole Vegas saga is apocryphal. Conceivably, he spent the weekend in Reno. Or skiing at Tahoe. Or on the beach in Waikiki.

Countless theories abound, all unproven. What is known, for certain, is this: Bobby Kennedy showed up in Jake's office. At seven forty-five on a Monday morning. He told Jake he was broke, that he needed a job, and he persuaded Jake to hire him by using magic. Moreover, he arranged for Jake to pair him with a guy who was utterly lacking in scruples, and who had, in the past, been known to spin a good yarn, although not always good enough to fool the jury.

But his criminal record is irrelevant. Except insofar as it underscores the fact that he was always on the lookout for a scam. And that when it came to higher principles, he didn't have any. Which is to say, he was the sort who'd write a book just for money. And for a chance to go on Oprah and sip fine sherry. Or to put it in a nutshell, the guy was a hack; a hack Bobby Kennedy could exploit. A hack who could be used because he wanted to be used.

Bobby sold him on the project in half a day. In fact the hack was so greedy that Bobby didn't have to sell, at least not in the traditional sense. He didn't have to make a pitch or twist his arm. He merely had to show him several minor parlor tricks. E.g., the simple levitation of a dresser. And the transmogrification of a glass of water into beer.

The mark took the ball from there. Yes, he thought up the book on his own! Or so he believed as he asked Bobby questions, as he pumped and probed and dug for more details.

But enough about who used who and to what extent. The point is, Bobby's legacy was secure. He knew his story would be told, and by a masterful huckster. It was bound to reach the people someday.

And once that was settled—once the rogue heard the tale and was convinced of its profit potential—Bobby turned his attention to the more important matter of saying farewell to his friends.

Bobby did it on a Wednesday afternoon. It was a raw, gloomy day. It was spitting snow.

Bobby and Mitch and Full-Time John and Special Ed and Bobby's partner were on their way down to Newtonville. That's a far-off one-horse town by Mount Rainier. They were heading for the town's grammar school. They were delivering a piano, a spanking-new Baldwin upright.

This was a very big event for the school. An assembly had been scheduled to mark the occasion. The local notables had been invited to attend.

Still—major capital expenditure for Newtonville or not—the delivery was a three-man job. Even two men with experience could've done it. So why had Jake dispatched *five* men? Plus one extra truck for the two extra men?

To this day, he doesn't know what possessed him. Squandering labor and equipment like that. Passing up billable hours! Saying no, as he'd done—as he'd had no choice but to do—when a blue-chip account had called.

The call came at one forty-five. It was from a big downtown law firm. They were in a jam. They were so desperate for help they offered time-and-a-half for several men to assist with moving files. Yes, time-and-a-half during regular hours. Which meant the guys who did the work would never know. Which meant that Jake could've pocketed the difference himself!

Provided the job got done. But sadly for Jake, it didn't. He was forced to turn it down because he lacked the resources, because the bulk of his fine crew had gone to Newtonville.

Such shameful waste can drive a business owner crazy. Which is why, even now, months after the fact, when he can't fall asleep at night, Jake sits up and wonders what happened. What got into his head that day? And he wonders, as well, why only four men returned. Five went down but four returned.

That fucking Kennedy.

It was Kennedy who didn't come back. He *disappeared,* say the guys. Yeah, he vanished down there.

Jake suspects some monkey business, and he is right. Bobby *did* cast a spell to make Jake send them all down, and Bobby had a good reason: it was convenient. He could be with his friends for the whole afternoon. He could give them some quality time. He'd have a chance to fill them in on his adventures in the joint, and he could treat them all to burgers, shakes, and fries.

But to return to the events at that remote grammar school: after lunch, the moving convoy arrived. And the fat, jolly mayor of the town was there to greet it. He heartily shook hands with all the guys. And he insisted that they stay for the exciting assembly. He said the children would be thrilled to see real movers. And extremely disappointed if the movers didn't stay.

Well, what could they say to that?

"Far be it from us to let the little darlings down. Provided we get paid," said Special Ed.

"Well aren't *you* a card," said the mayor to Ed, as he clapped him, rather forcefully, on the back.

Then the principal stepped forward. He had bad posture. And a severe case of dandruff. And even worse breath.

He shook hands in a limp, sad man's way.

The guys shook his hand back, then took the piano off the truck and walked it into the school auditorium.

The students and the teachers were waiting. They were sitting in those hard fold-out chairs. At a sign from the principal they lamely applauded the arrival of the new piano.

After this, the glum principal introduced the fat mayor, who gave a twenty-minute basic rah-rah speech. Next, the PTA president gave a speech. And the presidents of the Lions, the Rotary, and the Kiwanis—each of them stood up and gave a speech.

There were some scattered allusions to the importance of music, but mostly the piano went unmentioned. Instead, the speakers dwelled on loyalty and pride, honoring the flag, and all that crap.

The kids were bored silly, of course. So they yawned up a storm. And they fidgeted. And neglected to keep their hands to themselves. Or their feet on the floor. Or their eyes up front. Some of the bold ones even talked to their neighbors, which caused their teachers to say "Hush!" in loud stage whispers.

Bobby stood by the wall with the other moving men. He saw a melancholic fourth-grade girl. And a depressed little boy, a dorky kid with thick glasses who was sitting in the fifth-grade row. And who, predictably enough, was the target of spitballs. Bobby watched him take a steady stream of hits.

Bobby sighed and looked away. He closed his eyes. And for the first time in a while he really missed his own kids. Not that they were kids anymore. They were adults in the world who had kids of their own. Except for David, Bobby thought. Except for David.

He remembered his dead little boy. He remembered a spring afternoon. It was the spring after Jack was killed.

He'd come home for a nap of all things. Yes, he, Bobby Kennedy, the tireless Bobby, had left the office at two. Just wandered off. Without saying a word about where he was going or when he'd return.

He didn't care. He was fed up with life and he hated his job, now that no one was calling him back. Lyndon Johnson ignored him. Edgar Hoover ignored him. Governors and senators ignored him. Even if they came from unpopulous states, from states with no clout, they ignored him. Even if they came from fucking Wyoming—in fact *especially* if they came from Wyoming—they went out of their way to not call Bobby back.

Bobby understood. It was politics. See, in order to stay on Lyndon Johnson's good side, you had to keep a healthy distance from his enemies. And Lyndon's number-one enemy was Bobby Kennedy.

So people didn't call back, which was degrading. And to add to Bobby's woes, there was that Warren Commission. The results were still pending, and he was worried. What if, God forbid, they told the truth about Jack? About his nonstop White House orgy? About the mob connection? About the way in which Jack and, to some extent, Bobby had compromised the country with their peckers?

But no more about the Kennedy peckers! They can't be responsible for everything. All I'm trying to say is that Bobby came home in the middle of a spring afternoon.

It was a warm, muggy day. Baseball weather. Or so it struck Bobby when he saw his son David sitting on the broad front steps. Sitting and thinking his secret pensive child thoughts.

Bobby chucked his little boy on the chin. "Want to play catch?" he said.

David grinned, but then he got a troubled look.

"It's okay. You'll do fine," Bobby said.

"I know," David said. But he looked scared.

"It's okay if you drop the ball."

"I know," David said.

"Don't you want to play catch?"

"I do," David said. And he did. David *lived* to play catch with his daddy. And he didn't mind dropping the ball. He knew that Daddy understood when he dropped it. But what Daddy didn't know was that he had a new fear. He was afraid of getting *hit* by the ball. Of missing completely so that the ball hit his face. Or his arms. Or his legs. Or the worst place.

"I'll go get the gloves," David said.

He ran into the house and got the gloves from the closet where they kept all the sports equipment. Then it was on to the bathroom for the towels. There were a number of sizes to choose from. He stuffed a couple of small ones up his sleeves. And used a big one to cover his tummy. And forced some thin cotton towels down the legs of his pants. And put a thick one in front of his wiener.

He emerged from the house with the gloves.

Bobby looked at his towel-stuffed son.

Bobby didn't know what to do.

"I won't hurt you," he said.

"I know," David said.

"I promise to throw it real soft."

"I know," David said.

"So will you take out the towels?"

David tried to look puzzled. "What towels?"

Well, this was too much. Something snapped. Something usually reserved for dirtbags like Hoffa. Or for lazy assistants. Or for Chester Bowles. Something having to do with worry and grief and Mafia hitmen and Lyndon Johnson. Not to mention the fuckheads from fucking Wyoming.

"The towels in your pants!" Bobby yelled. "And the damned sissy towels in your shirt! Don't you *ever* lie to me. Is that understood?"

"Are you going to hit me?" David said.

"Am I going to *what*?" Bobby said.

"You can hit me if you want to," David said.

Bobby gazed at his puffed-out son.

Bobby realized that he wanted to hit him.

Bobby covered his face with his hands. "Oh my God," Bobby thought. "Jesus Christ, God forgive me."

"It's okay to hit me," David said.

Bobby opened his eyes and looked around. He spotted the sad little girl. He spotted the sad little boy. He surveyed the roomful of bored, tired children.

The last speaker droned on.

The speaker finished.

The students and teachers got ready to leave.

Bobby acted on the spur of the moment. "Hold your

horses!" he said. "Just a minute!"

Bobby strode to the front of the room. Bobby stared at the brand new piano. Bobby caused it to rise several feet in the air. He let it linger for a moment. He put it down.

For the first time that day, the kids were impressed. Their applause was sincere.

Bobby bowed.

Then he stared at the piano again. The keys started moving at a furious pace. The piano was playing by itself! It was playing a passage from "Rhapsody in Blue."

Even the grownups were impressed. Especially the ones who were familiar with Gershwin, who knew how difficult it is to play him well.

And Bobby Kennedy wasn't missing a note. Or glossing over the intricate three-on-two rhythms.

The passage ended with a syncopated flourish.

Bobby bowed like a world-famous maestro. He blew a kiss to the crowd.

What a ham!

The audience roared its approval. Everyone, it seems, was having a blast, except for the poor flustered principal. Bobby's nonsense was disrupting the afternoon schedule. It would wreak havoc with the teachers' lesson plans. So the principal had to do something, and he had to act fast. But before he had a chance to make his

move—before he could stand up and shoo Bobby out—
the mayor put a hand on his arm.

You see, the mayor understood that the kids were
enthralled, and that they'd go home after school and tell
their parents. Moreover, since the mayor owned the
town's only paper, he could expect—indeed contrive—
a favorable write-up. Yes, the locals would read about
the great magic show the mayor had arranged for *at no
cost*. Which is just the sort of news, during tight fiscal
times, that can secure a nice handful of votes.

"Cool your jets," the mayor said to the principal.

"But Jim—" said the principal.

"He's harmless. He's good."

"But—"

"Just shut the fuck up!" the mayor said.

Bobby winked at the mayor and continued. He left
magic behind and moved on to stories: funny stories,
strange stories, true stories.

He told a story about a chicken named Matilda. And
another about a dog named Roy Cohn. The dog named
Roy Cohn was a coward. He was such a coward, in fact,
that when Roy was a puppy and heard his own bark for
the first time, he ran under the house and hid for three
days.

The children laughed about the coward, Roy Cohn.

And about a cat named Marcello who was very aggressive, especially when it came to hunting birds. He loved killing so much that when a sparrow flew by, Marcello lunged from a third-floor window.

"Did he die?" asked a boy.

"No, he's fine," Bobby said. "Marcello always lands on his feet."

"But did Marcello catch the bird?"

"Marcello *always* gets his bird."

"He *never* misses?"

Bobby smiled. "Would I kid you?"

Then he turned his attention to the sad fourth-grade girl.

He gazed into her mind.

He told a story.

It was about a little girl who got yelled at and teased and even beaten by her mean foster daddy.

The little girl's name was Alexandra. Which, as it so happens, was the name of the girl who was sitting in the fourth-grade row.

She started listening intently to Bobby's story. To his account of all the beatings she'd endured. Of the beatings she'd received for not getting straight A's. Or for spilling her milk by mistake. Or for having to pay a school-library fine. Or for not washing the dishes fast enough. Or, more often than not, for no reason at all.

"That's right, for no reason," Bobby said. And he went on to explain that Alexandra was shy, that she had a hard time trusting others. But she managed, in school, to reach out to one girl. Yes, she actually made a real friend. And one day at lunch she worked up the courage to ask her friend over to play. And her new friend agreed. She came over!

This was a wonderful thing, a momentous event. Nothing like it had ever happened to her before.

But wouldn't you know, on that day of all days, her fat foster daddy left work early. He came home early and drunk from the office. And he started to cuss at and beat Alexandra in front of her first and only friend.

Who, of course, had never witnessed such horrible rage. And who ran from the house, sobbing wildly. She was so frightened, in fact, that even in school, she never spoke to Alexandra again.

Bobby sighed and looked around at all the scared, quiet children. They were waiting for the story to change. They were sitting and hoping for a nice, happy ending.

Bobby shrugged. "Life is like that sometimes."

Then he smiled at the sad little girl. And he smiled at

the sad fifth-grade boy. And at the jittery principal. And at the agitated mayor, the very agitated overweight mayor. Who wasn't pleased with this stranger who seemed to know a great deal about his fourth-grade foster daughter, Alexandra.

The mayor glowered at Bobby in classic Jimmy Hoffa style. He wished that Bobby would simply vanish from the earth.

"Be careful of what you wish for," Bobby cautioned the mayor.

Then he turned to his moving-man buddies. And he talked to his friends with his thoughts. "I have to go now," he said. "But I'll always be here. I'll always be watching for you."

"Like Oriet?" Mitchell said.

"Like Oriet," Bobby said, as he raised his arms to heaven and disappeared.

AFTERWORD by Stanley V. Higgins
A Note On Veracity

It has not escaped the attention of this author that a tale such as this one—fraught as it is with levitations, alchemical transformations, episodes of extrasensory cognition, and related thaumaturgical phenomena—is likely to raise questions of veracity in the minds of judicious readers. It is conceivable, therefore, that some of you who are both inquisitive by nature and not without financial resources may, at this very moment, be contemplating a pilgrimage to Seattle for the express purpose of seeking out corroborative sources. And while I always have and always will wholeheartedly endorse that most noble of endeavors—the gallant pursuit of truth—it is incumbent upon me to forewarn any would-be zetetics of potential unanticipated pitfalls.

If, for example, your quest leads you to the loading dock of the Jake Fuller Moving Company, you may find Mitchell Bromberg and "Full-Time" John Trefethen to be less forthcoming than you might wish. Indeed, if, after introducing yourself, you launch into a series of questions regarding such matters as Bobby Kennedy's temporary shrinkage of oversized bookshelves to make them fit into undersized elevators, or his vanishing act down in Newtonville, Washington, these normally gracious and most genial of moving men are likely to respond with icy stares, folded arms, and unwavering, even hostile, silence. That, at least, is the behavior I observed when strangers who'd heard rumors of a wonder worker in our midst began, in the late winter and early spring of 1990, to trickle into the warehouse at the rate of two or three per week.

Since both Mitchell and Full-Time John had, in their conversations with me, been voluble on the subject of Bobby Kennedy, I was, I must say, mystified by their deportment. Until, that is, Mitchell pointed out that as an "insider"—one who'd witnessed the miracles firsthand— I represented no threat to their reputations. Whereas, he continued, for all he and Full-Time John knew, these ostensibly well-meaning "outsiders" might be media spies. Yes, that's what he labeled them: spies. Spies, moreover, who would like nothing better than to make us all out to be a bunch of crackpots; who would, in fact, relish the opportunity to increase the size of their news-papers' circulations, or of their respective viewer or listening audiences, by holding Jake's entire crew up to public ridicule and scorn. In short, Mitchell seemed to be saying, it is better to err on the side of prudence than to risk excoriation by the fourth estate.

Being all too familiar with the journalistic mindset myself—and to its unconscionable distortions of my past encounters with the law—I not only sympathize with Mitchell's position: I salute his good sense and foresight. Indeed, it is almost as if a wisp of Bobby Kennedy's extraordinary political acumen rubbed off, like so much static electricity from a balloon, on Mitchell Bromberg's soul. But be that as it may, I do not think the inquiring reader will get what he or she wants from Mitchell or Full-Time John.

As for that most engaging tertiary source, "Special Ed" Granack, he is, alas, no longer with the company, and I have no forwarding address. This state of affairs is truly unfortunate because, as opposed to his cohorts, fear of being thought a fool never prevented Ed from saying or doing anything. Yet, as you may well have already surmised, it is this same reckless disregard for the opinions of others that led to Ed's dismissal from Jake Fuller's employ a mere week before my own termination. There is no need to recount all the unpleasant details, to depict Jake in high dudgeon, and so forth.

Suffice it to say that if a moving man drops his end of a credenza in front of said credenza's owner; and if, as a consequence, one of the credenza's legs breaks off, it is not terribly politic for the moving man to pick up the leg and wave it about as if it were some drunken cowboy's pistol. Furthermore, the situation will only be exacerbated if, while brandishing the ersatz pistol beneath the customer's nose, the moving man utters the following sentence: "I swear they make this particle board sh— just to f—k the f—k—g movers!"

My apologies, of course, for Ed's language.

With regard to Loretta Easton, her book store is located just where Bobby Kennedy said it was: at the corner of Fourteenth and Pine, across from the Second Congregational Church and adjacent to the American Artificial Limb Company. Ms. Easton herself is a striking, buxom, auburn-haired woman who favors long, colorful parrot-shaped earings, and who exudes the sort of raw sensuality to which few males—and certainly no Kennedy male—could be completely immune. I personally found her braided armpit hair to be exotic, suggestive, for some odd reason, of wild zebras cavorting on the veldt, an image that served, in my own mind, at least, to underscore Ms. Easton's abundant reserve of primal sexual energy. Bobby Kennedy, as you know, had a different response to the armpit hair. But that, as they say, is what makes horse racing.

In any event, I am sorry to report that Ms. Easton was disinclined to assist me with my research. Indeed, on my fifth visit to the store, when I finally came clean, so to speak—admitting that I did not, as I'd earlier claimed, have an abiding passion for books on semiotics by French philosophers, but had actually been frequenting her establishment in the hopes of obtaining anecdotal information about an individual named Bobby Kennedy—Ms. Easton's nostrils flared, her turquoise eyes blazed, and she referred to her former escort as a sexist egress from which solid wastes are excreted by the body. Or words, at any rate, to that effect.

Under the circumstances I cannot, in good conscience, encourage others to seek Ms. Easton out. Unless, of course, they are the types who derive pleasure from receiving expletive-laden tongue-lashings. And as for that potential motherlode of corroborative data, the Washington State Reformatory in Monroe, I should warn you, first of all, that the prison's relative proximity to the city notwithstanding, it is a "1" call from Seattle. And if, in spite of the expense, you elect to telephone the institution and to make inquiries about a former inmate Kennedy, a reported plague of beagle puppies in the big yard, and/or the outcome of disciplinary proceedings involving one Clarence "Gerbil" Foley, you are likely to be transferred from the switchboard operator to the desk sergeant; from the desk sergeant to the shift lieutenant; from the shift lieutenant to an administrative secretary; and, ultimately, to a certain Associate Warden Carnahan. At each point along the way you will be required to explain, in complete detail, the purpose of your call, and at each point along the way you can expect to be put on hold for upward of five minutes. Thus, it would behoove the wise caller to have a book or a magazine handy.

Once you are connected with Associate Warden Carnahan, you will discover that he asks you many more questions than you ask him; you will hear a number of disconcerting clicks and buzzes on the line, and when, at long last, he has extracted all the information you possess—and, presumably, recorded the conversation for posterity—he will politely inform you that it is the policy of the prison to make no comment on matters pertaining to internal security.

That, at any rate, is what happened to me. And it was all on my nickel, no less!

But to get back to the subject at hand: the question of this tale's veracity. How, in view of the aforementioned obstacles, should the inquisitive reader proceed? My advice, for what it's worth, is to spare yourself the inconvenience of a trip to the remote and oft-gloomy Pacific Northwest, and to simply *choose* to believe that Bobby Kennedy returned. After all, when one considers the improbability of creation; the incomprehensible nature of time, space, nothingness, and infinity; the genius of Mozart; the myriad insoluble mysteries of the universe, in short, is it not easier to believe than not believe in miracles?

Certainly it is. Or so say I, Stanley V. Higgins. But then, I am at an advantage here, for I saw Bobby's wonders with my own eyes. You have already heard, *ad nauseum*, about the levitated dresser. And I have alluded to that late Tuesday afternoon when—after a bitch (if you'll excuse me) of a household move, replete with heavy, unwieldy pieces; a narrow and curve-riddled staircase; and a notably peevish customer—we made, at Bobby's suggestion, a post-job pit stop at MacDonald's. As I watched my partner scarf down his fourth and fifth Big Macs of the day, I found myself wishing that the cup of ice water I'd ordered was, instead, a tall mug of dark German beer. Which, thanks to Bobby's intervention, is precisely what it became. He may have performed the feat to satisfy my craving. Or perhaps he did it (gratuitously, if that's the case) to reinforce my curiosity about his essence. On the matter of Bobby's motive, you must draw your own conclusion. With regard to that mug of beer, however, I can report with certitude that no deity ever tasted a finer cup of ambrosia.

Which brings us to that final and most dramatic of Bobby's miracles: the ascension down in Newtonville. The students, teachers, and child-abusing mayor responded as you might expect: with gasps of puzzlement, delight, consternation, and/or indignation. What is far more revealing, however, is the response the deed elicited among Bobby's intimate moving-man colleagues. They were saddened, profoundly saddened, by his ascension. But neither Mitchell, Special Ed, nor Full-Time John exhibited so much as a *hint* of shock or surprise.

Clearly, they had anticipated something like this. Clearly, Bobby's magic wasn't novel to them. And it was this absence of astonishment, more than anything else, that served to convince me that my cognitive abilities were fully intact; that the events I'd witnessed over the past three days had not been, as I'd vaguely feared, a simple case of synaptic dysfunction brought about by prior experimentation with a veritable host of mind-altering substances.

During the ensuing weeks and months, I learned much from Bobby's friends. More, even, than I have recorded in the preceding narrative. I learned, for example, that early on in Bobby's moving-man career (Bobby's frequent displays of wizardry notwithstanding), Mitchell expressed skepticism about his identity. "I heard Bobby Kennedy was ruthless," Mitchell is reported to have remarked one day. "You're too nice a guy to be Bobby. You act more like a reincarnated Adlai."

If the comment was intended to provoke, it was nothing less than a resounding success. Bobby pouted, grew sullen, and finally snarled at Mitchell, "Let's play some football after work." So at a quarter past five they drove over to the playing fields just south of Green Lake, and joined in on a civil, gentlemanly pickup game of two-hand touch. Or what had *been* a civil game until then. It seems that Bobby proceeded to mortify Mitchell and to alienate his teammates and opponents alike by tackling instead of tagging, interfering on pass defense, and flagrantly cheating on out-of-bounds calls while challenging anyone who disagreed with him to a fist fight.

Following this thoroughly reprehensible perfor-
mance, Mitchell had to concede that Bobby Kennedy
was who he said he was; that Bobby Kennedy was an
SOB after all.

And while I'm on the topic of reprehensible behavior,
it is perhaps worth noting that in the aftermath of
Bobby's tiff with the exotic Loretta Easton, his aforementioned chronic tardiness and cavalier treatment of Jake's
expensive equipment were among the *least* of his of-
fenses at work. For, according to my sources, it was
during this trying time that Bobby's fancy breeding
reared its ugly visage, manifesting itself in a disgraceful
exhibition of diction-based snobbery. Apparently, Bobby
badgered even his most trusted associates about their
usage of standard moving-man terminology.

Why, Bobby demanded, was furniture never
"moved" but rather "humped"? Why, Bobby railed,
did his cohorts insist on "blowing" the chairs on and
"blowing" the chairs off, instead of "loading" and "un-
loading" them from the truck? And why, in God's
name, were work surfaces forever being "zipped,"
"slapped," "slammed," and "knocked" into place, instead of being "screwed in" to office panel systems?

When I asked Special Ed about Bobby's attitude
toward nouns, Ed replied that Bobby made fewer com-

plaints about them. Still, Ed acknowledged, on more than one occasion Bobby did point out that desks were desks and bed frames were bed frames, not "suckers" or "puppies" or "deals."

From a grammarian's standpoint, of course, the late senator's observations were not without merit. For whatever the reason, moving men rarely utilize any variant of the verb "to move," but are far more likely to speak of "scooting those pups into place" (i.e., wheeling the files to the corner) or of "busting the deals off the rig" (i.e., carrying the credenzas off the truck). Nevertheless, as Bobby Kennedy undoubtedly knew, his compatriots were not about to alter their speech patterns in such a manner as to conform to the examples set by Bobby's own stodgy headmasters decades before in New England. Consequently, Bobby's petulant and condescending outbursts served only to irritate and insult those very individuals who might have consoled him in his hour of need; who might, if he'd given them half a chance, have dissuaded him from committing a felony.

But all that is water over the dam (if you'll forgive the cliche). Besides, it is conceivable, perhaps even likely, that Bobby's destiny was foreordained. Yes, the Fates carry us whither they will, which, in his case, meant a soul-burnishing journey to an isolation cell at the Washington State Reformatory, and in my case, as you know, led to Montana.

What you do not know, however, is that before I drove to Kalispell, I stopped briefly at the university in Missoula. I did not do this—as I might have in my randier days—for the frivolous purpose of striking up a conversation with; drinking in the scent of; appreciating the curves of; and, with any luck, enjoying a fleeting dalliance with a delectable and intellectually engaging coed. And perhaps it's just as well that flirtation was not on my agenda. After all, in this, the age of the Politically Correct, to admit to such designs, or, for that matter, to the mere possession of hormonally triggered mating urges, is practically a capital offense.

But don't get me started on that! Don't get me going on that most insidious strain of Orwellian thought policing that has embedded itself, like a malignant tumor, in the once-vital and fluid academic left, and which, if not excised soon, will turn the great political continuum into an ignoble political circle where, at the apex, the ailing and rigid far left, and the forever mindless religious right, will meet, join hands, and perform a foul dance in honor of their Vishnu, Cotton Mather.

No, don't get me started on that! Suffice it to say that I went to Missoula on a purely scholarly mission. I was hoping that a visit to the library would satisfy my curiosity regarding several minor inconsistencies. And I was not disappointed. As I suspected, based upon my strong lay background in the minutiae of public affairs, my former partner's account of himself was occasionally at odds with recorded history.

To wit, while it is true, as Bobby told me, that he had, at one point, challenged Jimmy Hoffa to a pushup contest outside a Senate hearing room, Bobby had not, as he claimed, introduced himself to Hoffa by suggesting a physical altercation. Rather, it was gangster Joey Gallo to whom, at their initial meeting, Bobby was heard to say, "So you're Joey Gallo the Jukebox King. You don't look tough to me. Wanna fight?"

Mr. Gallo—who was well known in mob circles for executing his adversaries by impaling them on meat hooks—demurred on the grounds that he firmly subscribed to nonviolent resolution of conflicts.

And again, while it is true, as Bobby told me, that he held a tense discussion with Martin Luther King on that perilous night when the great leader and his supporters were trapped inside a Montgomery church; and that, in a moment of frustration Bobby testily referred to the expiration of the late Kelsey's gonads; it is not true, as Bobby asserted, that when he complained about the way in which the Alabama situation was proving to be a political embarrassment for the president, Dr. King responded by stating, "We've been embarrassed all our lives." Those memorable words were uttered, at a later date, by Dr. King's assistant, Reverend Abernathy.

Moreover, while it has been documented that Bobby's dog, Brumus, lifted his leg and made water on a guest at a Hickory Hill lawn party, the guest was not, as Bobby informed me, the ambassador to France, but, rather, the wife of a low-level diplomat.

And as for that infamous big-time footsie incident with Marilyn Monroe, it did indeed take place backstage at Madison square Garden. But the year was 1962, not 1961.

Now in fairness to Bobby Kennedy, these and other trifling discrepancies can be easily explained away. Bobby had, after all, spent the better part of two decades out of the loop, so to speak; the better part of two decades off in purgatory. Furthermore, he may well have been addled by the horrors he'd endured at the Washington State Reformatory. Under the circumstances, one can certainly excuse a few mix-ups on names and dates.

This having been said, however, there was one omission in the story Bobby told me that no amount of trauma or lapsed time can explain, that can only have been deliberate on Bobby's part. For, as I learned on my sojourn to the university library, historians have now determined, beyond a shadow of a doubt, *that Marilyn Monroe was not his only mistress.* To be sure, she was the most significant of Bobby's paramours, in part because of the extraordinary level of passion she aroused in then-Attorney General Kennedy, and in part because of the potentially disastrous political repercussions that the affair, had it gone public, would have generated. And, it should be noted, not even Bobby's harshest critics have dared to suggest that the extent of his philandering in any way compared to that of his brothers or satyrical father. Nevertheless, to put it bluntly, he screwed around.

But what of it, I thought, as I drove north from Missoula in a recently purloined blue Chevy, skirting the shore of the resplendent Flathead Lake and squinting in the glare of a vermilion sunset. If the Gods saw fit to forgive Bobby Kennedy, then why, at long last, shouldn't we?

Select Bibliography

Collier, Peter and Horowitz, David
The Kennedys, an American Drama. Warner Books, New York 1984.

Goodwin, Doris Kearns
The Fitzgeralds and the Kennedys. St. Martin's Press, New York 1987.Select Bibliography.

Griffiths, Philip Jones
Vietnam Inc.. Collier Books, New York, London 1971.

Guthman, Edwin 0. and Shulman, Jeffrey, eds.
Robert Kennedy In His Own Words. Bantam Books, New York, Toronto, London, Sydney, Auckland 1988.

Lasky, Victor
Robert F Kennedy: The Myth and the Man. Pocket Books, New York 1968.

180

Halberstam, David
The Unfinished Odyssey of Robert Kennedy. Random House, New York 1968.

Plimpton, George, ed. and Stein, Jean, interviewer
American Journey: The Times of Robert Kennedy. Harcourt Brace Jovanovich, Inc., New York 1970.

Scheim, David E.
Contract on America: The Mafia Murder of President John F. Kennedy. Shapolsky Publishers, Inc., New York 1988.

Schlesinger, Arthur M., Jr.
Robert Kennedy and His Times. Ballantine Books, New York 1978.

Spada, James
Peter Lawford: The Man Who Kept the Secrets. Bantam Books, New York 1991.

Steinem, Gloria
Marilyn. New American Library, New York and Scarborough, Ontario 1986.

Robert Ellis Gordon lives and writes in Seattle, Washington. He has worked as a moving man for many years, and has taught fiction writing in the Washington State prisons since 1989.